GOTCHA!

by the same author

A Higher Form of Killing (*with Jeremy Paxman*)

GOTCHA!

The Media, the Government and
the Falklands Crisis

ROBERT HARRIS

faber and faber
London & Boston

First published in Great Britain in 1983
Published in the United States in 1983
by Faber and Faber, Inc., 39 Thompson Street,
Winchester, MA 01890
Printed in the United States by
Vail-Ballou Press, Inc., Binghamton, New York

Library of Congress Cataloging in Publication Data

Harris, Robert, 1957–
   Gotcha!: the media, the government, and the Falklands crisis.

   Includes index.
   1. Falkland Islands War, 1982—Journalists.
2. Falkland Islands War, 1982—Censorship—Great
Britain.   3. Government and the press—Great Britain.
4. Censorship—Great Britain.   I. Title.
F3031.H36   1983   997'.11   83-1695
ISBN 0-571-13052-6

Contents

Acknowledgements	*page*	9
Dramatis Personae		11
Introduction		13
1. Pens and Bayonets		15
2. All at Sea		26
3. Bingo/Jingo		38
4. Nott the Nine o'Clock News		56
5. The Enemy Within		73
6. The Ministry of Truth		92
7. From Our Own Correspondent		120
Conclusion		148
Index		153

Acknowledgements

I would like to record my thanks to Douglas Millar, Clerk to the House of Commons Defence Committee; Kenneth Derbyshire, Director of the Audit Bureau of Circulations; the Institute of Practitioners in Advertising (for permission to quote from the National Readership Survey); Simon Jenkins of the *Economist*; Pat Kavanagh of A. D. Peters. Laurence Rees gave me great help and support. Willa Hancock showed me loyalty and kindness above and beyond the call of duty.

I would also like to thank Christopher Capron for granting me permission to start writing this book; and my editor, David Lloyd, who was generous in giving me the leave which enabled me to complete it.

My greatest debt is to those, both in government and in the media, who talked to me about their roles in the crisis. Most asked me not to name them. I respect their wishes and give them my thanks.

December 1982   R. H.

Dramatis Personae

On board *Invincible*

Alfred McIlroy	Reporter, *Daily Telegraph*
Gareth Parry	Reporter, *Guardian*
Michael Seamark	Reporter, *Daily Star*
Tony Snow	Reporter, *Sun*
John Witherow	Reporter, *The Times*
Roger Goodwin	Ministry of Defence Press Officer

On board *Hermes*

Brian Hanrahan	Reporter, BBC television
Michael Nicholson	Reporter, ITN
Bernard Hesketh	BBC cameraman
John Jockell	BBC sound recordist
Peter Heaps	ITN engineer
Peter Archer	Reporter, Press Association (later replaced by Richard Savill)
Martin Cleaver	Photographer, Press Association
Robin Barratt	Ministry of Defence Press Officer (later replaced by Graham Hammond)

On board *Canberra*

Patrick Bishop	Reporter, *Observer*
Ian Bruce	Reporter, *Glasgow Herald*
Leslie Dowd	Reporter, Reuters
Robert Fox	Reporter, BBC radio
Max Hastings	Reporter, London *Standard*
Charles Lawrence	Reporter, *Sunday Telegraph*
Martin Lowe	Reporter, Wolverhampton *Express and*

	Star (later replaced by Derek Hudson of the *Yorkshire Post*)
Robert McGowan	Reporter, *Daily Express* (joined at Ascension Island)
Alastair McQueen	Reporter, *Daily Mirror*
David Norris	Reporter, *Daily Mail* (joined at Ascension Island)
Kim Sabido	Reporter, Independent Radio News
John Shirley	Reporter, *Sunday Times*
Tom Smith	Photographer, *Daily Express* (joined at Ascension Island)
Jeremy Hands	Reporter, ITN
Robin Hammond	ITN cameraman
John Martin	ITN sound recordist
Alan George	Ministry of Defence Press Officer
Martin Helm	Senior Ministry of Defence Press Officer
Alan Percival	Ministry of Defence Press Officer

Introduction

The *Sun* prints all of its 4 million copies in London and as a result is the first national newspaper in Britain to go to press. On the night of 3 May 1982, with most of its journalists on strike, the paper was produced by its management aided by a handful of non-union staff.

These are the two reasons advanced by the editorial director of Rupert Murdoch's News Group Newspapers to excuse what was probably the most famous headline of the Falklands war: 'GOTCHA!', used to describe the sinking of the Argentine cruiser, the *General Belgrano*. 'I agree that headline was a shame,' he says. 'But it wasn't meant in a blood-curdling way. We just felt excited and euphoric. Only when we began to hear reports of how many men had died did we begin to have second thoughts.'

A few minutes after eight o'clock that evening, the first copies began coming off the presses. By the time Kelvin MacKenzie, the paper's editor, had remade the front page, the whole of the first edition—upwards of 1,500,000 copies—was already on its way to the north of England, Scotland and Northern Ireland, bearing witness to the *Sun*'s initial 'excitement and euphoria'. In subsequent editions, a more subdued headline, which the *Sun* apparently believed better in keeping with the sombre news was used: 'DID 1200 ARGIES DROWN?'

Such was the brief life and abrupt death of a headline which has nevertheless secured its own place in the history of the Falklands war.

'GOTCHA!' both epitomized and, as it turned out, marked the high point of the tide of jingoism whipped up by Fleet Street. The day the headline appeared Britain suffered her first major loss when HMS *Sheffield* was destroyed. The darker side of jingoism is a paranoid tendency to blame defeats on subversion at home. The BBC, the *Daily Mirror* and the *Guardian* were accused of 'treason' by the *Sun*, taking its cue from the Prime Minister, who deplored the BBC's failure to identify itself more closely with 'our boys' on the task force. It was the start of an uncomfortable week for the Corporation, which culminated in its Chairman and present Director-General being howled down by half the Conservative Party in the House of Commons.

A reaction set in. The attack on the broadcasters was followed in the latter half of May and the first half of June by a ferocious counter-attack in which Fleet Street joined, aimed principally at the Ministry of Defence. Six weeks of anger and frustration in London over the lack of information and television pictures were compounded by growing evidence of wholesale bungling by the Ministry of Defence with regard to the task force correspondents. The charge was led by the BBC's Assistant Director-General: 'The miscalculations of the handling of the information war are, I suggest, a better target for back-bench wrath than the BBC,' he wrote on 3 June. A week later the House of Commons Defence Committee obliged by announcing its intention of holding an inquiry into how Whitehall handled the coverage of the conflict.

This book is based on the written and oral evidence collected by the Committee and on interviews with the leading protagonists in the 'information war'. Whereas the Committee confined itself specifically to the record of the Ministry of Defence, I have added two other aspects: the coverage of the war by Fleet Street, particularly the tabloids, and the political row surrounding television output.

What follows is an account of the power of information and the struggle to control it which took place in April, May and June 1982. The implications of *this* fight may yet prove more important than those of the real war in whose shadow it was fought.

1. Pens and Bayonets

The night-duty press office at the Ministry of Defence is a claustrophobic room on the ground floor, furnished with four telephones, a television, a shabby wooden cupboard and a small bed. Its lightly dozing occupant in the early hours of Friday, 2 April, was a public relations officer of many years' standing called Roger Goodwin.

For more than six hours he had been answering calls about a rumoured invasion of the Falkland Islands and telling news agencies and night editors that London had heard nothing. At 2 a.m. the telephone rang again. Pulling on a pair of trousers and still wearing his pyjama jacket, Goodwin made his way to the fifth-floor naval operations room to be briefed by Admiral Sir Henry Leach, the First Sea Lord. Leach, just returned from Downing Street and dressed in a dinner jacket, announced that it now looked certain that an invasion would take place that day. Six hours later, just after 8 a.m. London time, Argentine troops went ashore on the Falklands.

Goodwin and his colleagues in the Ministry press office spent the day that followed in a state of siege. Ten public relations officers manned thirteen telephones and dealt with what one called 'a tidal wave' of inquiries from Britain and abroad.

> We could tell what time the world was waking up. The first wave of calls came from Britain and Europe early in the morning. Then, at lunchtime, Canada and America—first the east coast, then the west. By the end of the day it was Japan, Australia and New Zealand. . . .

Almost all were requests for places on board the naval expedition being mobilized in Portsmouth. 'We got requests from people who wanted to sail with the task force from Dallas and San Francisco. I remember one man demanding to go who worked on the *Rocky Mountain News*.' All the requests were added to a central list, which

15

by the time the fleet sailed contained hundreds of names submitted by over 160 separate organizations. According to another press officer, there were 'around twenty requests for accreditation from the BBC alone'—from individual programmes, from the World Service, from the Pebble Mill Studios in Birmingham, 'from some people who said they worked for the unit that made *Sailor* and who wanted to make a documentary about life aboard the task force...' Some requests were bizarre, including one from Roddy Llewellyn, the former escort of Princess Margaret.

The Ministry of Defence's problems were made worse by the fact that they had little idea of what was going on. Demands for confirmation of the rumoured invasion could only be met with the blanket statement that there was 'no information available'. Two hundred yards away across Whitehall, the Foreign Office was still undecided about whether or not an invasion had taken place.

In the House of Commons, MPs were clustered round news agency tape machines which were quoting claims from Buenos Aires that Port Stanley had been seized. But at 11 a.m. in the Chamber, the deputy Foreign Secretary Humphrey Atkins assured MPs that no invasion had taken place. 'The report on the tapes comes from an Argentine newspaper. We were in touch with the Governor half an hour ago and he said that no landing had taken place at that time.' At 2.30 p.m., the Leader of the House of Commons, Francis Pym, rose to tell MPs once again that the situation was unchanged. It was not to be until six o'clock in the evening, ten hours after the landings on the Falklands, that the Government finally confirmed that the islands had been seized. For anyone seeking information it was a day of frustration and confusion—a foretaste of the chaos that was to come.

It is an axiom of military planning that in time of war the interests of the armed forces and those of the media are fundamentally irreconcilable. The regulations later issued to the task force correspondents put it succinctly: 'The essence of successful warfare is secrecy. The essence of successful journalism is publicity.' Of the three services, the Royal Navy is traditionally the most wary in its dealings with the press. Life on board ship is an enclosed, secretive world. Unlike the Army in Northern Ireland, the Navy has had little experience in handling the modern media. The fact that the Falklands war had to take the form of an 8,000-mile naval operation with a limited land battle at the end of it meant that from the media's point of view there were bound to be problems from the outset.

Preparations to send a task force to liberate the islands in the event of an invasion had begun on Wednesday, 31 March, supervised by Sir Henry Leach in consultation with the Fleet's Commander-in-Chief, Sir John Fieldhouse. Significantly, the more politically attuned Chief of the Defence Staff, Admiral Sir Terence Lewin, was at that time in New Zealand. On Friday morning, an hour after the invasion, when the Ministry of Defence asked how many journalists would be allowed to sail with the task force, the answer which came back from Fleet Headquarters at Northwood was: none. When the Ministry insisted that to exclude the press totally was unthinkable, the figure was grudgingly changed to six, and then increased to ten, including a television team. The Navy's attitude was summed up by Leach, who wanted to know whether he was expected to load his ships with 'pens or bayonets'.

The man in charge of dealing with the media in the Ministry of Defence at this time was not a PR specialist but a career civil servant. Ian McDonald was later to achieve fleeting international stardom as the Ministry's official spokesman, but his natural habitat is Whitehall's undergrowth of committees and non-attributable briefings, hidden from view. McDonald was completing an attachment as Deputy Chief of Public Relations; previously he had been concerned with the Ministry's recruitment and salaries. When the Falklands were invaded, McDonald was acting head of the department. Not until 13 April did the new Chief, Neville Taylor, arrive, and the gulf in responsibility and personality between the two men was to become an important element in the Ministry's handling of press relations during the war.

McDonald's initial plan—one which would, in retrospect, have avoided many of the major problems which were to follow—was to have the correspondents fly out to Ascension Island and join the task force there, midway through its voyage to the South Atlantic. This would have given the media and the armed forces two precious weeks in which to organize and to reach agreement as to how any military action should be reported. But again, the Navy proved unco-operative.

Despite the fact that reporters could have been landed in total darkness and escorted off the island immediately, despite the fact that the Navy would have had total control over communications, there was, said one MoD man, 'a total, total ban on any movement into Ascension' on the part of the press. Sir John Fieldhouse explained later:

> What I was concerned about was that people should get out of the aircraft and see that there was no air defence at Ascension. There were no missiles protecting that airfield at that time. There was no reason why a frogman could not have got out of a rubber boat on the coast and walked straight in amongst all these aircraft and planted demolition charges without any difficulty at all, such· was the enormous activity around.

With this option ruled out, there was no alternative but to get the correspondents on board before the fleet sailed—and by Sunday morning, after a weekend spent arguing with the Navy, McDonald had less than twenty-four hours left.

'Had anyone deliberately set out to confuse the issue,' Brian Hitchen, the London editor of the *Daily Star*, later wrote, 'they could hardly have been expected to do a better job than the Press Office at the Ministry of Defence on 4 April 1982.' To the *Guardian*, the arrangements for the accreditation of correspondents to the task force were 'rushed and confused'; to the *News of the World* 'complete chaos'; to *The Times* 'peremptory and short-sighted'; to Max Hastings of the London *Standard* 'dogged from the outset by the resolute opposition of some parties in the Royal Navy and the Ministry of Defence to taking correspondents to the South Atlantic at all'.

McDonald convened a meeting at the Reform Club in Pall Mall, of which he is a member, attended by the editors of BBC Television News and ITN, and by an assortment of technical experts. It was agreed that the two organizations would each be allowed to send one correspondent; that they would share the same cameraman and sound recordist; and that an engineer would sail with the fleet to test the possibilities of transmitting pictures back to London. With television taking up five places, this left a further five to be divided up among the press.

The Director of the Newspaper Publishers' Association (NPA), John Le Page, was just settling down to Sunday lunch at his home in Essex when the telephone rang.

> I thought it was probably someone ringing to tell me about some industrial dispute, but it turned out to be a press officer from the Ministry of Defence telling me that the task force was going to

sail early the next day and it was essential that any correspondents wanting to sail with it arrived at Portsmouth by midnight that evening. They wanted the NPA to nominate the names of who was to go. In order to arrange accreditation the Ministry said they would have to receive the names within the next four hours.

Abandoning his lunch, Le Page spent the next ninety minutes telephoning almost every newspaper in Fleet Street: all insisted that their correspondents should be allowed to go. 'The only thing I could do was put all the names in a hat and let my wife draw the winners. It sounds incredible, but what else could I do?' Mrs Le Page picked the *Daily Mirror*, the *Daily Express*, the *Daily Telegraph* and the *Daily Mail*. Le Page had already agreed with the Ministry of Defence that the fifth place should go to the Press Association.

This was the beginning of what Le Page describes as 'hell: the worst day I've ever had'. With the lines almost constantly engaged, it took him almost an hour to get through to the Ministry of Defence and give them the result. Once it became known among the remaining four national daily and eight national Sunday newspapers that they were to be given no facilities aboard the task force, Le Page's telephone began ringing, and for the remainder of the day he fielded calls from company chairmen, managing directors and editors.

The disappointed newspapers launched a violent lobby to get their own reporters accredited to the task force. Sir Frank Cooper, the Permanent Under-Secretary at the Ministry of Defence, was rung up at home by, among others, the news editor of the *News of the World*. 'We stressed that we wanted to go and were promised that someone would call the news editor back at home. He received no calls. . . . He found the MoD unhelpful and, we suspect, obstructive.' Pressure was brought to bear upon the Defence Secretary, John Nott; the Scottish newspapers—totally excluded, along with the foreign and provincial press, from the NPA draw—lobbied the Secretary of State for Scotland. As one senior MoD official put it: 'Whoever had strings to pull was pulling them.'

The decisive intervention came from 10 Downing Street. Bernard Ingham, the chief press secretary to the Prime Minister, had already spent most of Friday and Saturday nights talking to editors. On Sunday, the whole weight of the press's disappointment and frustration was brought to bear on Downing Street. The *Daily Star* was one of a number of papers which wrote directly to the Prime Minister:

> I believe you will be horrified to learn that the *Daily Star* and three other national daily newspapers, *The Times*, the *Guardian* and the *Sun*, have been excluded from sailing with the naval Task Force on the ludicrous grounds that there is not enough room aboard the ships.
>
> Please help us to be there when Britain's pride is restored by the armed might which you promised the nation.
>
> Only you can give the order to have the name of our writer, Michael Seamark, included on the Ministry of Defence sailing list of accredited correspondents which is being closed tonight.

It has now entered the mythology of Fleet Street that, in the words of the *Star*, 'had it not been for the direct intervention of the Prime Minister . . . half the British Press would have been waving the Task Force goodbye from the quayside.' In fact, Bernard Ingham intercepted all letters and messages before they reached Mrs Thatcher, who was preoccupied with other matters, and without consulting her he instructed the Ministry of Defence to ensure not only that more reporters went but also that they comprised a more representative group. The mere flourishing of Mrs Thatcher's name was enough. The Royal Navy gave in.

There were now approximately six hours left before midnight, the deadline by which correspondents had to report to Portsmouth, and reporters had already begun converging on the naval base.

'I was told', recalls the BBC's Brian Hanrahan, 'about one o'clock on Sunday to be down in Portsmouth by eight o'clock that night.' Michael Nicholson of ITN was on a walking holiday in the Lake District when his office caught up with him at 2 p.m. on Sunday afternoon and told him to go straight to Carlisle, where a light aircraft was waiting to fly him south; he was in Portsmouth by 7 p.m. Tony Snow was told that evening by his paper, the *Sun*, 'that I should "head towards Portsmouth" and telephone when I got near'. At 8 p.m., Michael Seamark of the *Star* was still at the Ministry of Defence, fruitlessly trying to obtain accreditation; at 10 p.m. he finally received permission to join the task force and drove south furiously, abandoning his car in Portsmouth. Gareth Parry of the

Guardian was at home when his office rang at 9.30 to tell him to be in Portsmouth by midnight, leaving him forty-five minutes to catch the last train. 'He just happened to be there,' said his editor, 'and he leapt on to a train carrying a sweater and a paperback.' *The Times* only heard that their reporter, John Witherow, had a place at 10.15 that night.

Little more notice was accorded to the press officers selected to accompany the journalists on the task force. Two MoD public relations men were told at lunchtime on Sunday that they would be sailing the next day: Roger Goodwin, whose normal job is dealing with press matters for the Navy, and Alan Percival, formerly the PR officer for the Ulster Defence Regiment. The third and most senior member of the trio who originally sailed with the task force was the Navy's deputy head of public relations at Fleet Headquarters at Northwood, Robin Barratt.

The allocation of press officers and journalists to particular ships was decided by the Navy at Northwood, and the slowly expanding list of correspondents showed the extent of the ground it had been forced to concede. Originally no places had been set aside for journalists, then on Friday there were six, on Saturday ten, and now, after pressure from Ingham—and also from Nott, who told the Navy it was a political, not a military matter—the total had reached fifteen, comprising two photographers, a BBC cameraman and sound recordist, an ITN engineer and ten reporters.

Gradually word about who had been given places spread among the journalists crowded in Portsmouth's Holiday Inn. The BBC's Robert Fox, hoping to cover the war for radio news and the World Service was told that he wouldn't be going; so too was Kim Sabido of Independent Radio News, who discovered that his place had gone to the ITN engineer Peter Heaps (Fox and Sabido were both given berths, later in the week, on the *Canberra*). Of the few who were to sail the next day, Gareth Parry (*Guardian*), John Witherow (*Times*), Mick Seamark (*Daily Star*), Tony Snow (*Sun*) and Alfred McIlroy (*Daily Telegraph*) found themselves assigned berths on board HMS *Invincible* with Roger Goodwin. The television team—Hanrahan and Nicholson, together with cameraman Bernard Hesketh, soundman John Jockell and engineer Heaps—were put aboard the flagship, HMS *Hermes*, along with the Press Association (PA) reporter Peter Archer and the PA photographer Martin Cleaver; the accompanying PRO was Robin Barratt. David Norris of the *Daily Mail* was placed alone, and unattended by anyone from the MoD, on the Royal Fleet Auxiliary *Stromness*.

The most aggrieved pair were Robert McGowan and Tom Smith, respectively reporter and photographer for the *Daily Express*. To their disgust they found themselves confined to a logistics landing ship, the *Sir Lancelot*, due to slip away quietly twenty-four hours after the rest of the fleet. McGowan complained both to the *Express* office and to Alan Percival, the PR man assigned to travel with them; it was hopeless. 'There was no appeal,' he wrote bitterly afterwards. 'We were told to take it or leave it.'

Early the next morning, the correspondents were given a last chance to call their families before the warships moved off, *Invincible* leading the way, at 10.15. Many were still exhausted by what the *Daily Mail* later called the 'mad scramble to secure places' of the previous forty-eight hours. Behind them lay a weekend of chaotic last-minute phone calls, interrupted plans and desperate journeys. Ahead of them lay—what? None could have anticipated that they would spend more than six weeks at sea, a large part of that time under air attack; or that they would become part of Britain's first major amphibious assault since D-Day; or that they would be expected to ·dig their own trenches, cook their own rations and generally survive on their own a gruelling three-week campaign: none of this was foreseen. The general attitude was summed up by the editor of BBC television news, who dispatched Brian Hanrahan to the South Atlantic with the words, 'You've just had a sailing holiday. How about another one?'

Gareth Parry was one of the reporters who was to have a particularly grim campaign. He is a veteran war correspondent, with twenty years' experience covering conflicts in Africa, the Middle East, Cyprus and Vietnam (where he lived for a year); yet he had never encountered anything like this.

> I genuinely thought we'd be sailing for a couple of days around the Isle of Wight; maybe if we were very lucky we'd get to the tropics. I couldn't conceive of the idea that we were going to war in such an old-fashioned way. It's extraordinary that even today nothing can apparently be settled without hurling large amounts of explosive at one another.

Parry's attitude was typical. 'See you in a week' had been another editor's parting remark to his task force correspondent. Patrick

Bishop of the *Observer* recalled how one group of journalists—who were to sail with the second contingent of the task force later that week—'held a sweepstake on the date when the ship would turn to come home. My bet was it would be within a week. The longest was 27 May.' In the same spirit Robert McGowan bet Alan Percival £5 that they wouldn't see a shot fired in anger.

The armed forces are prepared for war; journalists are not. Most were too young even to have remembered, let alone endured, National Service. Yet arguably the Falklands was to require greater physical and mental readiness than any war covered by the media in recent times. The haphazard way in which journalists were selected and sent on their way, in most cases without even the most rudimentary equipment, could easily have proved fatal. As it was, three reporters returned home before the fighting was over, and at least one appeared to be visibly distressed when recalling his experiences.

The military sent a psychologist with the task force to study the reactions of men under the stress of war. He stated at the outset to one Ministry official that in his view the press would prove a 'weak link'. Perhaps the same thing would have happened if the reporters had joined the fleet at Ascension, as McDonald had originally proposed. But the reporters would then have had a clearer idea that it was no 'sailing holiday' that they were letting themselves in for.

The journalists on *Hermes* and *Invincible* were followed four days later by a further thirteen aboard the requisitioned liner-turned-troopship, *Canberra*. This brought the total to twenty-eight and represented a crushing victory by Whitehall over Northwood. Indeed, there is today a general belief in the Ministry of Defence that although initially too few journalists were to be allowed to join the task force, in the end there were too many. As Sir Frank Cooper told MPs four months later: 'There is no doubt in our minds—and this may surprise you, but I am going to say it now—we had more people with the task force than we could properly cope with in the light of the conditions on the ships and on land.' And one senior official recalls: 'We were pressing the Navy to take the largest possible number of reporters without any real idea of what we were getting into.'

The four extra days given to prepare the *Canberra* did little to ease the confusion which had marked the departure of the carriers. Securing a place was still a matter for string-pulling and special pleading, frequently spiced with a little discreet blackmail. Ian Bruce of the *Glasgow Herald* was there thanks to 'pressure from MPs favourable to the cause of Scottish press coverage' (i.e., one suspects, Scottish MPs in the Glasgow area). Max Hastings of the London *Standard* relied upon everybody he knew 'in political circles who might have any influence whatsoever upon the Minister of Defence or the Ministry of Defence'. Leslie Dowd of Reuters owed his inclusion to the 'considerable pressure' applied by his agency to Sir Frank Cooper. It took 'impassioned pleas' from the BBC and ITN, together with the personal intervention of John Nott, to get a three-man television team aboard *Canberra*. They were finally granted their places less than six hours before the ship sailed.

What, meanwhile, of the foreign press, whose calls had swamped the MoD's press office on the day of the invasion? No provision was made for them at all. Sir Frank Cooper now admits, 'With hindsight, we probably ought to have had one or more representatives of the foreign press,' but he adds, 'They were singularly disinterested right at the start.' Like most journalists, claims one Ministry official, 'they simply couldn't believe that the whole business wouldn't be sorted out by Al Haig and the UN.' This is unfair. What really happened was that, lacking the necessary domestic political influence, the foreign press were unable to follow up their initial requests with calls to the MoD from MPs, Cabinet Ministers and ennobled newspaper proprietors. As a result, they failed to secure a single place, leaving Reuters as the only 'international' organization on board the task force. 'The addition of just one other organization,' claimed Michael Reupke, their editor-in-chief, 'would have made this a genuine news operation rather than appearing a British propaganda exercise.' It was a short-sighted error on the part of the Ministry of Defence, one which could have been avoided and which did considerable damage. The Foreign Press Association called the MoD 'indifferent' to the world's media, and claimed that 'the negative image which the Falklands conflict elicited in some foreign newspapers must to some extent be ascribed to that indifference.'

Yet, given the hostile reception at that time being accorded to the *British* reporters by the Royal Navy, it was perhaps fortunate that there were no foreign papers on board. Relations froze even before the *Canberra* set sail. On the night before she left, Alastair McQueen of the *Daily Mirror* was having dinner with a senior Ministry of Defence press officer at Southampton's Post House Hotel, when a

Royal Navy commander icily told him: 'There is no room for you. We do not have the proper accommodation for you and you would be much better staying back here in the UK. You are only taking up space we could put to much better use.' McQueen felt that 'he seemed to have the impression that journalists were demanding officer-standard accommodation. Our only aim was to accompany the forces.'

Strict, security-conscious, conservative and facing the prospect of a dangerous operation which would leave very little margin for error, most naval officers viewed the imminent arrival on board of a mob of undisciplined, unfit, metropolitan civilians with something approaching disgust. 'The Navy's idea of PR', says one MoD man, 'is to get the mayor and the local newspaper editor on board and give them pink gins in the wardroom.'

Captain Chris Burne, the senior naval officer on *Canberra*, initially refused point-blank to have the media on his ship and had to be ordered to his face to do so by Captain Tony Collins, dispatched to Southampton by the Ministry of Defence to oversee the embarkation of the journalists. Burne retaliated by assigning the reporters to the worst accommodation on the ship—the Goanese crew quarters—and there they would have remained, at least according to some MoD press officers, had it not been for the intercession of the chief public relations officer accompanying the task force, Martin Helm. (Two weeks later Burne is said to have tried to have Helm removed for constantly badgering him with requests on behalf of the press.) After this inauspicious start, the ship sailed on Good Friday, 9 April.

As *Canberra*, *Invincible*, *Hermes* and the rest of the force headed towards the Falklands, they already had stowed on board all the problems which would later dog the coverage of the war. The Navy was hostile and aggrieved at being overridden. Some of the reporters, in the rush to get places, were not physically or psychologically prepared for what lay ahead. The media representatives as a whole, correctly suspecting that they were with the fleet only on sufferance, were ready for a fight. As for the Ministry of Defence, it had twenty-eight representatives of the press at sea with no clear idea of how their copy could be vetted, what disruption its transmission would cause to the Navy or what political problems lay in store at home. . . . Only later in the crisis, when successive diplomatic initiatives had failed to find the expected solution and the fighting began, did the strains inherent in this fragile situation really show.

2. All at Sea

Before embarking, the task force correspondents filled in accreditation papers so old that they contained passages in Arabic, relics of the Suez adventure twenty-six years before. The correspondents promised 'to submit for censorship all books, articles, or other material concerning the task force during the period of operations and to abide by the decision of the censorship authorities concerned'. The grounds for censorship were to be strictly military ones. Before *Canberra* left, Captain Tony Collins gave a lecture to the journalists. 'He told us', recalls Kim Sabido, 'that there would be no way our material would be censored for things like style or taste. If a marine got into a fight with a para, and even if one of them was killed—well, fine, we could report it.'

Strict guidelines governing what the press could report were laid down by Sir Frank Cooper at a meeting held on 7 April with the editors of the national media. These stressed the need 'to maintain strict security' and were sent to the task force commanders:

> Officers and crews of ships with embarked correspondents should be reminded of the standard rules for dealing with the press and are to be specifically briefed to avoid discussing with them or in their hearing the following:-
> a. Speculation about possible future action.
> b. Plans for operations.
> c. Readiness state and details about individual units' operational capability, movements and deployment.
> d. Details about military techniques and tactics.
> e. Logistic details.
> f. Intelligence about Argentine forces.
> g. Equipment capabilities and defects.
> h. Communications.

All such details were to be removed from correspondents' reports.

Journalists rarely submit easily to censorship, but the rows which followed the issuing of the MoD's guidelines went far beyond the sort of disagreements which might have been expected.

The men charged with the main burden of imposing censorship were the Ministry of Defence press officers accompanying the task force, the 'minders' as they became known. Upon these luckless civil servants the press later vented ten weeks of pent-up grievances and bitterness.

In Michael Nicholson's view,

> these men were not only unqualified, they were unwilling to help. They were afraid: they were looking over their shoulders: they were constantly worried about London.

> I found the MoD PRs lazy [wrote Tony Snow], loath to agree to do anything that involved them having to do any work; obstructive ... and dishonest—I was lied to by them on a number of occasions.

To Alastair McQueen they seemed

> unable to drag themselves away from the cossetted environment in which they normally deal with defence correspondents. They were totally unequipped for a wartime role. They did not understand the requirements of newspapers, radio or television organizations. They had absolutely no sense of urgency or news sense. They had absolutely no idea of deadlines or how to project a story to obtain the maximum impact. In my opinion they were completely out of their depth.

Even before the task force sailed, their presence aroused violent impulses. Gareth Parry recalls how, a couple of minutes before *Invincible* left Portsmouth, he and some other journalists on board saw their minder, Roger Goodwin, making a last-minute call from a telephone box on the quayside:

> There was a coil of rope lying nearby, and the ship was literally about to sail. We all looked at one another. Have you ever imprisoned anyone in a phone box with a length of rope? You should, it's very effective. In retrospect we would have saved ourselves an awful lot of bother.

It is scarcely surprising that three months after the end of the war, the minders still had about them a furtive, hunted air, like minor criminals on the run.

Their position was an invidious one, sandwiched as they were between a set of newspaper journalists instinctively hostile to interference and naval officers who—with a few honourable exceptions—appear to have regarded the media as little better than an Argentine fifth column. 'Our role in the end was as whipping boys between the press and the Navy,' says one minder. 'We helped get rid of the worst excesses of both sides.' To Sir Frank Cooper, they were 'the hinge on which the door was going to grate however much oil was put on it'.

There were five minders with the fleet, their day-to-day task being to take the reporters' copy, check it to ensure that it did not breach any of the guidelines laid down by the Ministry, have it cleared by an officer on board ship and then arrange for its transmission back to London. In addition to Roger Goodwin, Alan Percival and Robin Barratt, there were a further two PROs, Martin Helm and Alan George, on board the *Canberra*.

Roger Goodwin, a heavily built man, married, with a long record in public relations in Cyprus, Hong Kong and Germany, was to become a particular butt of press criticism. 'It was felt,' wrote one editor, 'that his knowledge of Fleet Street deadlines was somewhat inadequate—possibly explained, I understand, by the fact that before joining the MoD he was an Agricultural Correspondent for a Midlands newspaper.' (Nicholson later claimed: 'They would say, "We understand your problems: we are ex-journalists ourselves," and we discovered they were night-subs on the *Mid-Somerset Chronicle* or something: they were mostly failed journalists rather than ex-journalists.')

Although *Invincible*'s captain, Jeremy Black, was initially well-disposed towards the press, the carrier was a nest of problems. Not the least of Goodwin's worries was the presence of Prince Andrew, a helicopter pilot on the same ship as reporters from the *Sun* and the *Daily Star*. From the moment Goodwin stepped on board, unaware of his narrow escape from incarceration at the hands of Gareth Parry, he was besieged with requests to interview the Prince. Like most officers, Andrew first learned there were to be reporters on board when he rounded a corner and saw a group of them. His first reaction was to ring Buckingham Palace and complain. He also sought out Goodwin, who had to advise him that having the press on board was something that the Prince, like everyone else, would have to accept. Tony Snow and Mick Seamark of the *Sun* and the *Daily Star* were told that it was 'not MoD policy' to give members of the Royal Family serving with the armed forces undue publicity. Undeterred, one of Snow's first dispatches, printed on the following Saturday (10 April) began:

> 'I HUNT THE ENEMY WITH ANDY'
> SUN MAN JOINS THE PRINCE ON
> SOUTH ATLANTIC COPTER PATROL
> I flew on a helicopter mission
> with Prince Andrew yesterday . . .
> to hunt down enemy ships.

Not until the fourth paragraph did the *Sun*'s readers learn that the Prince was actually flying a long way from Snow in 'a second helicopter covering a nearby section of the ocean'. The journalists were forbidden to approach Andrew, and it was the Prince himself who later broke the silence by coming over to the five *Invincible* reporters in the bar one evening and offering to buy them a drink.

As far as the tabloids were concerned, Prince Andrew was one of the major stories of the war. This made the lot of Robert McGowan, the *Daily Express* man confined to *Sir Lancelot*, all the harder to bear. He was unable to get near the Prince, and soon he had even more troubles. *Hermes* and *Invincible* had been seen leaving port; *Sir Lancelot* had not, and London therefore directed that its presence with the task force be kept secret. McGowan overcame this problem in finest Fleet Street tradition, telling *Express* readers mysteriously that he was on board 'HMS *Cinderella*—the Ship that Can't be Named'. Unfortunately, three days out at sea radio silence was imposed on the fleet. The carriers had secure communications enabling their reporters to carry on filing stories; *Sir Lancelot* had not and the ship that couldn't be named now also couldn't transmit. 'We were blacked out by radio silence,' moaned McGowan. 'No words or pictures could be sent by us for eight days on the way to Ascension Island.' He was later to say that he received more help from the Russians when he was covering the invasion of Afghanistan at the end of 1979 than he did from the British in 1982.

There were to be so many quarrels between media, minders and Navy during the empty week before the task force entered into actual operations that it is impossible to do more than pick out the key incidents. Initially, on *Invincible* at least, things did not go too badly. Captain Jeremy Black is something of a showman. 'A large, slightly balding man,' noted John Witherow of *The Times*, 'he had an American-style baseball cap with J.J. Black emblazoned across the back which he sometimes wore on top of his white anti-flash hood, and drank tea from a mug with "Boss" on the side.' Black is also one of those rare individuals, beloved by the media, with a natural ability to speak in headlines: he answered one question about whether the task force had passed the point of no return by telling reporters: 'There are no Rubicons in the South Atlantic.' Black told Goodwin that he believed it was right that the media should be accompanying the task force and promised to do everything he could to help them. He instituted regular daily briefings for the five *Invincible* correspondents. For the first two days these were on the record. But as Black was the only commander who was talking to the press in this way, he soon discovered he was dominating the coverage in London in a manner that was likely to annoy his naval peers. From 7 April the briefings became off the record; Black's words had to be attributed to 'a senior naval source'.

The *Invincible* journalists were lucky with their captain; the *Hermes* reporters were not. Michael Nicholson, the ITN reporter, said later:

> Captain Middleton did not like the press. He said to us from the very start that we were an embarrassment to him. He said, I remember, that it was not the first time he had been to war because he was at Suez but it was the first time he had been to war with the press and he was not looking forward to the journey. . . . He gave briefings for the first two or three days and that was the end of it. I got very friendly with a number of senior officers at commander-level and on one evening they confessed to me that they were outraged by a briefing they had had from the Captain in the few days after Portsmouth on our way out, in which they were told to be wary of us and that the information flow throughout the ship would be restricted because of our presence. They said it was the most disgraceful briefing they had ever encountered.

This briefing of Lyn Middleton's would appear to have been based on the signal received from the Ministry of Defence on 7 April directing task-force commanders to remind their officers of the 'standard rules for dealing with the press' and 'to avoid discussing with them or in their hearing' the classes of information regarded as unfit for publication. Later Nicholson believed that this determination not to reveal anything to the media on board—even though their dispatches were vetted anyway—led to the censoring of the ship's own daily broadcast of information to its company, the 'pipe':

> these pipes became less and less frequent and less and less informative and we were told by members of the wardroom that this was because we were aboard and that it was becoming embarrassing for information to be broadcast on the pipe because we were able to listen to it.

Officers and crew began to complain to the *Hermes* journalists 'that the ship was suffering from a lack of information because of our presence'. Hanrahan, Nicholson and the Press Association reporter Peter Archer, were driven to rely increasingly on sympathetic 'deep throats' among the ship's officers. Eight days out at sea, Robin Barratt, the minder on board *Hermes*, flew over to Roger Goodwin and arranged that his contingent of journalists should fly over to *Invincible* to do some filming and to record an interview with the more amenable Black.

Wednesday, 14 April, was a bad day for Goodwin. One of the features of the so-called 'information war' was that everyone fought everyone else: Whitehall fought the Navy, the Government fought Whitehall, all three fought the media, and the media, as 14 April demonstrates, fought among themselves. The *Invincible* journalists had survived for a week on a diet of unattributable briefings; now Black gave Hanrahan and Nicholson a television interview, something which is, by its nature, on the record. Archer of PA witnessed the interview, wrote a story based upon it quoting Black by name and dispatched it to London, thus scooping his competitors. When the *Invincible* journalists discovered this, there was, one eyewitness recalls, 'a blazing row in the wardroom'. This became still more heated when Nicholson discovered that a task-force helicopter had flown to Dacca in West Africa three days before to pick up an engineer from the garden of the British embassy to help repair a damaged gearbox on *Invincible*. So far no television pictures had been able to leave the fleet, and this would have been a perfect opportunity to send them back to London. Black had actually signalled

Northwood that he wanted permission to use the helicopter to fly back TV pictures but had received no reply. There were more complaints, more arguments, the outcome of which was that Black began privately referring to the press as 'the fourth form' and instructed Goodwin to ensure that Nicholson never came on board again.

Two days later, on 16 April, Black asked that all journalists' copy leaving *Invincible* should henceforth be cleared through his secretary, Richard Acland.

It was less than two weeks into the voyage and already the strain was beginning to show. The five *Invincible* journalists all slept in the admiral's unoccupied offices filled with filing cabinets. It was, recalled John Witherow of *The Times*, in *The Winter War*, 'rather like sleeping in a canning factory during an earth tremor':

> as the ship vibrated the files reverberated, as in an outlandish and off-key tintinnabulation. I tried sleeping with ear defenders and then with cottonwool earplugs. Neither was effective. We tried to locate the root of the noises, sticking sheets of paper between the cabinets—also with no success. Gareth Parry of the *Guardian* struggled naked over desk tops in the middle of the night, tapping the ceiling in a futile attempt to pinpoint a particularly irritating rattle. He retired to his camp bed muttering, 'Sleep is release. The nightmare starts when we wake up.'

On *Hermes* the press slept in the NAAFI's quarters; on *Canberra* conditions varied. Robert Fox and Kim Sabido shared a cabin— 'right in the bowels of the ship,' remembers Sabido, 'filthy and full of cockroaches. The loo kept flooding and the floor was awash with water. Mind you, Burne would've had us in the bilges if he could.'

'Emotionally', says Nicholson, who has covered fourteen wars, 'it was the worst thing I've ever done.'

For the broadcasters the problems were much greater than those encountered by the print journalists. Reporters on *Invincible* could at least stay on board ship, their copy transmitted via the carrier's communications centre. For Hanrahan and Nicholson, sending even a short voice dispatch to London posed enormous physical difficulties. Three days out from Portsmouth, when radio silence was imposed on the task force, dispatches had to be sent using a commercial telephone system known as MARISAT, carried on the

Royal Fleet Auxiliary *Olmeda*. Hanrahan and Nicholson would have to wait around on the deck of *Hermes*, sometimes for hours, until a helicopter could be found to fly them to the MARISAT ship. Often the journey would be made in heavy mist; at the end of it the reporter would be winched down, in heavy seas, on to the deck. There would generally follow another long wait before the satellite relaying the transmission could be contacted and a link established with London. Then, once the piece was read, the whole process of waiting, winching and flying would have to be repeated. 'Often you just went to your bunk hoping you'd never have to get out of it. You tended to get very tense, explode, say and do things which in normal times you wouldn't have done.'

The frustrations were compounded for Nicholson and Hanrahan by their belief that the Navy could have done something to ease the problem. Hanrahan heard that instead of their having to fly over to a MARISAT ship, voice communications were possible on a 'secure' line between the carriers and London; calls were even being routed along MoD telephone extensions. At first he was told by the Navy that this was impossible, 'but I later learned the link was used regularly, offered acceptable quality, and that voices could be recognized over it. To have recorded over that link would have saved much time (and wear and tear) for all personnel—and the helicopters.' Another method which would have cut out the waiting and the journeys would have been to use the ship-to-ship radio to speak from *Hermes*, through the MARISAT ship, and on direct to London. Yet, according to Nicholson:

> this was refused by Captain Middleton of *Hermes* on the grounds that the transmission would give away our position. Yet twice he gave us information this way because he wanted good news to get to London quickly. One instance of this was his telling us of the sinking of the *General Belgrano*.

With these frustrations and discomforts, personal relations inevitably became ragged. Nicholson, an impressively experienced and highly paid reporter, whom even his best friends would not describe as self-effacing, is said to have announced in the wardroom that he would be unable to live on the salary of a Rear-Admiral, a remark which was not well received. The BBC cameraman, Bernard Hesketh, accused (along with the other *Hermes* journalists) by one senior commander of being tantamount to an Argentine intelligence officer, 'pulled up his trouser legs and showed his wounds that he had got in France in the Second World War saying, "How dare you call me a spy? These are the wounds I got from the Nazis."'

For one man it all became too much. When *Hermes* reached Ascension Island, Robin Barratt, the senior PRO responsible for trying to keep the peace between the media and the Navy, was clearly suffering from something akin to nervous exhaustion. The head of public relations at Northwood flew out, saw him and immediately ordered him home—an indication of the state things were reaching. Barratt was the first but not the last victim of what Nicholson later confessed to be 'the overwhelming feeling which comes over one after a period at sea confined on a ship—irrationality, hostility, almost paranoia'. A short while later the MoD sent out a replacement PRO, Graham Hammond.

For some, however, the conditions served only to reveal hidden strengths. Brian Hanrahan emerged as one of the best-known reporters of the war, transformed, William Boot-like, from a man whom his BBC colleagues describe as a 'quiet, shy and unassuming' former stills clerk with a passion for amateur dramatics. 'Brian was extraordinary,' says one task-force colleague. 'The tougher it got, the cooler he became. A remarkable man.' Hanrahan knew virtually nothing about military matters; his ignorance was the key to his success. 'The advantage of being an innocent in these circumstances', he mused later, 'is that you tend to ask the questions the people back home would ask—"Why are they doing that? What effect will it have?"' It was Hanrahan's 'sense of wonder' at the power of modern weapons that helped him to convey the feel of the war to the general public.

Jeremy Black was becoming increasingly disenchanted with the press on his ship. Due to her engine trouble, *Invincible* arrived at Ascension after *Hermes* on 16 April. The ship's company was promptly informed over the pipe that its members would qualify for a Local Overseas Allowance of £4, but an hour or so later the Ministry of Defence decided against giving the men the extra money. There was, one official noted in his diary, 'extreme anger and upset' on board. Servicemen formed queues to complain to the journalists, who duly wrote dispatches about ill-will aboard the task force. The stories which resulted exasperated Black. He was unable, under the MoD guidelines, to stop the reports and did not attempt to do so, but he 'felt hurt and irritated'. Nor were the press feeling particularly amenable as, to their astonishment, London had refused to allow correspondents even to mention the fact that they were at Ascension. This was apparently done to avoid offending the Americans, 'although', as the BBC pointed out, 'the use of Ascension was common knowledge internationally, having been published in the USA'. It was also being discussed regularly in news bulletins in Britain, as the task-force reporters discovered to their chagrin a few days later, when newspapers and cassettes of TV programmes reached them.

Black's mood was not improved by growing complaints from *Invincible*'s communication officers that they were being swamped by press copy. Between them the five journalists were transmitting around 4,000 words of copy every day, with A. J. McIlroy of the *Daily Telegraph* writing particularly copiously (at one point he sent back four 1,000-word pieces in thirty-six hours). Already under orders from Northwood to keep its transmissions to a minimum, this meant that something like 30 per cent of the daily workload of the ship's communication centre was devoted to press reports. Goodwin soon began receiving written complaints from the officers involved.

Invincible's signals were processed through four visual display units, two devoted to incoming messages, two to outgoing. It was not, the main communications office informed Goodwin, simply a matter of telexing the stories and forgetting them. To send one press report would first take an operator an average of thirty minutes to transfer it to tape; it would then take time to link up with a satellite; frequently the message would be garbled in transmission, and London would ask for a repeat. In all, a single story could take between ninety minutes and three hours to reach London. At one time, *Invincible* had a backlog of 1,000 signals awaiting transmission.

Among these, on 19 April, were three which Black regarded as vital: one dealt with a piece of electronic warfare equipment that he urgently needed; the second was a request for a spare part for one of the ship's two missile radar systems, designed to alert the carrier to air attack; the third concerned a malfunction in the computer which guided the ship's Harrier jets into land. 'Passing out of the ship on that day,' claimed Black subsequently, 'and taking 30 per cent of my out-going traffic, as they did every day, was the [press] copy—some 3,500 words.' He quoted from one article:

The Page Three Girls are going to war. Fifty outsize pin-up pictures, each one 2 foot by 6 inches, were airlifted to the task force and are now on their way to the Falkland Islands. They were flown into Ascension Island, 4,000 miles from Britain, and then dropped by helicopter on to the *Invincible*. They were featured on a television show on the ship's closed-circuit television and then distributed so that there is at least one in every mess in the ship.

Black picked out another passage:

Skinhead Ian 'Walter' Mitty would put the frighteners on anyone. With his close-shaved head, tattoo-covered body and heavy bovver boots, he looks every inch what he is—a hard man. But Walter, 20, from Richmond, Yorkshire, was near to tears yesterday when he learnt that his dearest wish—to get at the Argies with his bare hands—had been denied.

('The youngest guys in the signals centre—I'm talking about kids of 19 or so—used to come and ask me why I kept giving them all this "dross and tripe" to transmit,' remembers one minder—an experience shared by most of his colleagues, both at sea and, later, on the Falklands.)

Black eventually insisted that press copy should be filed during the night, the slackest period for signals traffic. This meant that an average story would not appear until two days after it was written. A report compiled on a Monday morning, for example, would be likely to be transmitted in the early hours of Tuesday, missing the deadline for that day's paper and not, therefore, being printed until Wednesday. It was the press's turn to feel aggrieved, all the more so a few days later when Goodwin, on his own initiative and authority, limited each correspondent to a maximum of 700 words per day.

With tempers on board frayed, *Invincible* moved out from Ascension on the second leg of the voyage to the Falklands. The day she left, Alexander Haig's attempts to find a peaceful solution collapsed, and Gareth Parry's anticipated cruise around the Isle of Wight suddenly seemed a much more serious affair. Jeremy Black called a meeting of the journalists and told them that if any of them had any doubts or fears about their capacity to take what lay ahead, they should leave now, and he would arrange a flight from Ascension back to London. No one took up his offer. 'It suddenly seemed we had passed the point of no return,' wrote John Witherow, and he found that many of the crewmen were surprised they had remained. Almost everyone seemed to have believed that the press would abandon ship before things became dangerous. When the average sailor discovered the reporters had elected to stay of their own volition, 'they treated us either as deranged madmen or as warmongers. The next question would be along the lines of "I suppose you blokes are being paid a fucking fortune to be out here?" To deny it merely provoked disbelief.' On board *Hermes*, Brian Hanrahan found that the decision to stay broke down some of the reserve with which they had been treated. 'There was a great fear that we were going to go as far as Ascension, leave with a parcel of secrets and blab them out. Once it became clear that that was not the case, things improved a lot.'

Behind the carrier group came the amphibious landing force, centred on the troopship *Canberra*. Alan Percival, Robert McGowan and Tom Smith left *Sir Lancelot* and joined the main force on board the converted liner. So too did David Norris, who up to this time had been relatively free from interference. He wrote acidly afterwards: 'I was transferred, under protest, from *Stromness* to *Canberra* and into a morass of bureaucracy and acrimony.' Like their colleagues on *Hermes* and *Invincible*, all the pressmen chose to stay, with the exception of Martin Lowe, the reporter representing the regional press. Having seen the ship's doctors, he was evacuated to Ascension's Wideawake Airfield and flown home. 'When he went,' recalls Kim Sabido, 'we all said he was the sanest man among us.'

Depleted, aggrieved, frustrated, and in some trepidation, the minders and the media were borne south by the Navy to war.

3. Bingo/Jingo

Meanwhile back in London the Falklands war had enabled Fleet Street to indulge in emotions and language which had been denied to British newspapers for a generation. This was no shady adventure like Suez, no messy, drawn-out conflict like Ulster. 'The fleet sails now in restitution,' proclaimed the *Guardian* on 5 April. 'The cause this time is a just one.' On the morning that *Invincible* and *Hermes* left Portsmouth, *The Times* carried a massive leader entitled 'WE ARE ALL FALKLANDERS NOW': 68 column inches, more than 5 and a half feet, of authoritative prose rolling inexorably to its majestic conclusion:

> The national will to defend itself has to be cherished and replenished if it is to mean something in a dangerous and unpredictable world. . . .
>
> We are an island race, and the focus of attack is one of our islands, inhabited by our islanders. At this point of decision the words of John Donne could not be more appropriate for every man and woman anywhere in a world menaced by the forces of tyranny: 'No man is an island, entire of itself. Any man's death diminishes me, because I am involved in mankind; and therefore never send to know for whom the bell tolls; it tolls for thee.' It tolls for us; it tolls for them.

The *Daily Mail* spoke of the resurgence of national will in terms of 'the spring sun shining and the daffodils in full bloom' and warned:

> Forcing Argentina to disgorge the Falklands is a bloody, hazardous and formidable enterprise. It can be done. It must be done. And Mrs Thatcher is the only person who can do it. But she will have to show ruthless determination and shut her ears to the siren voices.
>
> If she flinches, if this bold venture fizzles out in vainglorious

bathos, Margaret Thatcher, her Government, and the Tory Party will be sunk.

Like the *Mail*, the *Guardian*'s leader writer also sought inspiration in nature:

> The time scale will stretch and stretch as fleets form and churn throughout April across 8,000 miles of the Atlantic. Easter, digging gardens, picking daffodils, will come and go. . . .

Having pronounced the task force 'just', the *Guardian* called in Churchillian terms on 'the ranks of Parliament' to 'contain their wrath and relish through the interminable weeks of impending conflict'.

Echoes of the war and of Munich were everywhere. In the *Daily Express* Lord Carrington and John Nott were 'Thatcher's guilty men. . . . They have misled themselves, the Cabinet, Parliament and the country. They have deceived everybody but the Argentinians.' 'If he has not the grace to resign,' said the *Mail* of Carrington, 'she should sack him.' 'Sack him and his whole rotten gang!' was the view of Andrew Alexander, the *Mail*'s political commentator: 'The plain fact is that the Foreign Office is rotten to the core, rotten with appeasement, rotten with real scorn for British interests ("narrow nationalism" they call them), rotten with duplicity. . . .'

Amid all these tolling bells, blooming daffodils and churning seas it was at first easy to miss the distinctively shrill note being struck by Britain's biggest-selling tabloid, the *Sun*. On 5 April, Carrington was caricatured as a mouse alongside Churchill as a bulldog. 'WE'LL SMASH 'EM!' was the banner headline on 6 April: 'Cheers as Navy sails for revenge'. Lord Carrington was the 'super-smoothie who became a scapegoat':

> HMS Carrington was finally sunk yesterday . . . torpedoed by over-confidence and wrecked by the humiliation of the Falklands disaster.
>
> And for Peter Alexander Rupert Carrington, 6th Baron and Foreign Secretary, his resignation was the inglorious end of more than thirty years in politics. . . .
>
> One of his scornful colleagues once told me: 'Carrington is okay. But when the chips are down, when difficult decisions have to be taken, he's either in Australia or chatting up some African chief.'

On the same day, the *Sun*'s editorial ('Show your iron, Maggie') took up a full page devoted largely to an attack on the Foreign Office:

> Since the days of Chamberlain, it has been a safe haven for the appeasers.
>
> ITS CODE has been that of the old Etonians and playing the game.
>
> ITS PHILOSOPHY has been: Never rock the boat. Never offend foreigners. . . .
>
> For ourselves, we do not care where it finds its recruits . . . provided they have fire in their bellies and a determination in their heart that no one is going to push Britain around.
>
> And that NOTHING comes ahead of the people of Britain, their lives, their prosperity, their future.
>
> The Iron Lady must be surrounded by men of iron!

Whereas the rest of the press generally abandoned much of its early rhetoric and concentrated over the next three or four weeks on the merits of the various peace proposals, the *Sun* sustained the same level of patriotic fervour. Indeed, it went much further. Although there had been violently patriotic papers in Britain before, this was the first time old-fashioned jingoism had been allied in wartime to a modern, mass-circulation British tabloid. All the new techniques of popular journalism—the massive, sloganizing headlines, the provocative comment, the presentation of news stories to buttress editorial comment—the whole box of tricks that was first perfected in the 1950s by the *Daily Mirror*, was employed by the *Sun* during the Falklands crisis. The results were among the most spectacular side-effects of the war.

Every weekday in Britain it is estimated that 31.3 million people read a national newspaper; on Sundays that figure rises to more than 33 million. Almost 80 per cent of British households see a national newspaper each day. One of the myths of the Falklands war is that the sales of newspapers rose dramatically during the conflict. In fact, there was little change. The market is already saturated and is thought to be incapable of further expansion. It is this salutary fact which has led to the present cut-throat circulation war, in which scarcely any of Britain's eight national daily and eight national Sunday papers are making a profit and in which each can hope to survive and prosper only at the expense of luring readers from a rival.

Of all the Fleet Street papers, the *Sun* over the past decade has proved the toughest competitor. Bought by Rupert Murdoch in 1969 from the Mirror Group, printed on his *News of the World* presses and pioneering the 'page three' picture of a topless model each day, the *Sun* has become a publishing phenomenon. Within eighteen months of taking over, Murdoch had doubled its sales. It outstripped the once unassailable *Daily Mirror* and by the mid-1970s was the largest-selling daily paper in Britain. Today, over 4 million people buy the *Sun*. Its readership is estimated to be 12.2 million; they are predominantly young (3.2 million are aged between 15 and 24) and lower-working class (9.3 million are in Britain's three lowest social classes, C2, D and E). It is a commercial success which underpins the Murdoch empire and which, in 1981, enabled him to buy Times Newspapers. (*The Times*, incidentally, is read—not bought—by 0.9 million people, of whom just *4,000* are in social classes C2, D and E.)

Only in the last two years has the *Sun* had any reason to worry. A precipitate price increase in the summer of 1980 caused sales to dip badly. The whole formula of the paper began to seem tired and stale. By the spring of 1981, the *Mirror* had caught up—and indeed for a few heady weeks may actually have overtaken its rival. The *Sun*'s problems were made more serious by the fact that its readership was being undermined by a new, brash tabloid, the *Daily Star*. The *Star*'s gimmick, playing on the British obsession with bingo, was each day to print a series of numbers which its readers could check off on special scorecards distributed throughout the country. Each week, the lucky readers with the right sequence of numbers won large cash prizes. 'It's a much better way of getting readers than advertising on TV,' says the *Star*'s London editor, Brian Hitchen. 'If you run a £500,000 advertising campaign on TV, you're very lucky if 2 per cent of the new readers stick with you. With bingo we were getting a sticking rate of 37 per cent.'

Murdoch moved swiftly to staunch the *Sun*'s loss of readers. 'We'd had a bad patch for about nine months,' says Peter Stephens, the Editorial Director of News Group Newspapers. 'We got off our backsides in the spring of 1981.' The *Sun* introduced its own bingo game, on a much bigger scale than that of the *Star*. Through the Post Office every home in the country received a supply of score cards. Massive prizes of £50,000 a week were offered. A national television advertising campaign was launched. The price of the paper was cut by twopence for ten weeks. The *Sun* put on 160,000 readers overnight, and within three months the paper had increased its circulation by 500,000 copies a day.

Having tempted the readers to buy the paper, it was now necessary to keep them hooked: to revitalize the flagging editorial content Murdoch decided to bring in a new editor. His choice was Kelvin MacKenzie, a ruthless 35-year-old with a generally acknowledged genius for Murdoch's brand of journalism.

MacKenzie had begun his rise as one of the *Sun*'s 'back bench'—the five senior sub-editors who decide the make-up of each night's paper. From this position he moved with Murdoch to New York to help in the restyling of the Australian tycoon's latest acquisition, the *New York Post*, a paper which was promptly driven relentlessly down-market in a vicious battle with the rival *Daily News*. He was lured back to London by a tempting offer to work on Lord Matthews's *Daily Express*, but after six months, says Stephens, 'we pinched him back.'

'Driving, youthful, modern-minded, brash' is Stephens's description of his younger colleague. 'A bit noisy, but the staff respond to this.' To a fellow Murdoch editor, Derek Jameson of the *News of the World*, MacKenzie is 'hardworking, almost a workaholic—he's in the office before everyone else, and often he won't leave until eleven at night. He's abrasive, ferocious.... His idea of relaxation is playing a few violent games of squash.' When the Queen asked Fleet Street editors to go to Buckingham Palace and discuss with her their coverage of the Princess of Wales, MacKenzie refused on the grounds that he was 'too busy'. He almost invariably refuses to give interviews; his reluctance is said to follow one broadcast in which, to the horror of News Group executives, he cheerfully admitted to being prepared to do anything to sell newspapers. ('I regret to say,' he wrote in July, 'neither myself nor any of our staff wish to talk about the way we reported the [Falklands] conflict.')

MacKenzie was successful in beating off the *Mirror*'s challenge. Whereas in April 1981 the *Sun* was selling 3,546,000 copies a day, in April 1982 the paper sold an average of 4,121,000; in the same period the *Mirror*'s circulation slipped back by 200,000. 'It's not a newspaper,' insists Mike Molloy, the editor of the *Mirror*, whose face seems to clench at any mention of the *Sun*.

It has no tradition or concept of itself. It's run by a proprietor who spends half his life on jumbo jets, and by a brilliant committee of marketing men. It's a technician's paper, a device for making money, with no pretensions to being anything other than ... [he breaks off, searching for a description] ... Christmas-cracker wrapping.

In order to keep up with the *Sun* and fend off the *Star*, the *Mirror* also introduced bingo; so did the *Daily Mail*. Not since the 1930s, when the *Daily Herald*, the *Express*, the *Mail* and the *News Chronicle* flooded the country with every imaginable free gift, from insurance to complete sets of Dickens, has the circulation war been fought more keenly or at greater expense. The *Sun*'s bingo promotion is said to have cost £3 million; the Mirror Group's £2.3 million. 'A massive poker game is going on in Fleet Street,' says Molloy, 'with bigger and bigger stakes. Sooner or later, something's got to give.'

The key to the struggle of selling newspapers, in the opinion of Derek Jameson, is to 'persuade the reader to break his habits':

Staying with a paper is an emotional commitment. He gets used to it. A paper strikes a chord in him. It's very rare in life that something comes along and persuades him to change it. One way might be bingo. Readers were changing papers at the rate of 100,000 a week thanks to bingo. Then along comes the war. War is an emotional business—blood, courage, guts, valour—it's something big enough to persuade people to change their paper. War and bingo.

It was against this background, in April 1982, that Fleet Street approached the Falklands crisis.

The *Daily Mirror* has been a supporter of the Labour Party since the war. In recent years, four of its senior executives have been given life peerages. Many of its editorial staff are Labour Party members. Like Michael Foot and the Parliamentary Party, the *Mirror* found itself caught between its dislike for Mrs Thatcher and its detestation of General Galtieri. The task force was a gamble, a venture so closely tied to the Prime Minister that on its success or failure depended her political future. What was the *Mirror* to do? On 5 April, it came out against using force in an editorial headed 'Might isn't right':

the main purpose of British policy now should be to get the best possible settlement for the islanders.

We could probably throw the Argentines out of the Falklands. But for how long?

Is Britain willing to spend hundreds of millions of pounds to keep in the area an army, navy and air force strong enough to repel any future invasion?

If it is, where is the money coming from? If it isn't, what happens to the islanders when we leave? . . .

The islands don't matter. The people do. We should offer each of them the chance to settle here or anywhere else they choose and we should pay for it.

What we must not do is promise to eject the invader and then desert them at some later date. The Argentine occupation has humiliated the Government. But military revenge is not the way to wipe it out.

Similar leaders followed, their titles alone conveying the consistency of the paper's line: 'A time for truth' (7 April), 'Time to stay calm' (8 April), 'Point of no return' (15 April), 'If all else fails . . .' (20 April), 'The dangerous hours' (23 April), 'Bleak outlook' (26 April), 'Keep on talking' (27 April). 'We wanted the whole thing sorted out by negotiations,' says Molloy. 'We were very cool about the task force.'

The *Mirror* was embarked on a dangerous path. When three national newspapers opposed the Government's handling of the Suez crisis in 1956, they lost readers heavily. The *Guardian* lost 30,000 in a matter of days, though it later recouped them. The *Observer* lost 30,000 in a week, fell behind the *Sunday Times* for the first time and never caught up again. It was the *Daily Mirror* itself which fared worst, losing 70,000 readers. The lesson appeared clear. Supported by Rupert Murdoch, who remained in daily contact with MacKenzie throughout the conflict, the *Sun* moved swiftly to corner the market in patriotism and to label its rival firmly as a disloyal defeatist.

The *Sun* had already attacked 'the sinking *Daily Mirror*' as a 'paper warrior' on 2 April, the day of the invasion. On 6 April it struck again. 'At home the worms are already coming out of the woodwork,' taunted the *Sun*.

The ailing *Daily Mirror*, which tried to pretend that there was no threat to the Falklands until the invaders had actually landed, now whines that we should give in to force and obligingly settle the islanders. But our whole experience with dictators has taught us that if you appease them, in the end you have to pay a far greater price.

'Once the war started, we were 100 per cent for it,' says Peter Stephens, himself a former deputy editor of the *Sun*. 'We had a black-and-white view of this war. It was us or the Argentinians. We had no dilemma about this.'

Other tabloid journalists were equally committed. 'Most people would've been pig-sick if there hadn't been a fight' is Brian Hitchen's analysis of the mood of the country. 'They wanted to get down there and beat the hell out of someone.' But even the London editor of the *Daily Star* was to find the *Sun*'s coverage 'over the top'.

'Youths demonstrated outside the Argentinian Embassy in London last night,' reported the *Sun* on 3 April. 'They sang "Rule Britannia", ending with "Don't Cry for me, Argentina, We're going to Nuke you".' 'Sack the guilty men!' ran the paper's editorial on the same day. 'What the hell is going on at Britain's Foreign Office and Ministry of Defence?' To oppose sending the task force was to be 'running scared'; on 7 April 'The Sun Says' fired this salvo:

> Out of the woodwork, like the political termite he is, crawls No. 1 Left-winger Tony Benn to demand the evacuation of the Falkland islanders. . . .
>
> And of course, he immediately wins backing from the whining namby-pamby ultra-Left, who always run scared at the first sign of a crisis.

The following day, the *Sun* printed a two-page spread of photographs of British marines surrendering on the Falklands. 'LEST WE FORGET' was the headline. 'This is why our lads are going to war.'

> These were the first moments of humiliating defeat for our brave Falklands few. It was a black moment in our history . . . a wound we cannot forget. But now our troops are on their way . . . to wipe out the memory and free our loyal friends.

The *Sun*'s attitude to a negotiated settlement was summed up in a five-word headline on 20 April: 'STICK IT UP YOUR JUNTA'. 'We urge every housewife NOT to buy corned beef produced in the Argentine' was the theme of an early campaign. Two days later the *Sun* reported that 'all over the country, families blacked the "bully" beef to show the South American bully boys what they thought.' 'Angry Sonia Lewis of Hockliffe, Beds.' was reported as saying:

'Refusing to buy corned beef is one way we Brits can show the flag.'

The average Argentinian—'Johnny Gaucho'—was reported as 'getting the jitters'. 'Several have stopped me', claimed the *Sun*'s David Graves in Buenos Aires on 7 April, 'and queried in trembling voices: "Will the British bomb Buenos Aires?"' Argentinians were 'Argies', a good target for humour. A daily series of 'Argy-Bargie' jokes was instituted, and soon the *Sun* was able to tell its readers, 'Your very own gags have been pouring in': 'They are so funny that we have decided to give £5 for every reader's Argy-Bargie joke published. Plus a can of Fray Bentos "non Argentinian" corn beef. Today's joke was told to us by Titus Rowlandson, 9, from Brighton. . . .' (Titus earned £5 for a joke about two British soldiers wiping out hundreds of 'Argy' soldiers.)

The *Sun*'s promotions department was equally busy. On 7 April, 'to give the lads a big morale-booster', the paper began distributing free badges bearing the legend: 'The Sun says Good Luck Lads'. (Derek Jameson was later seen wearing one at the Savoy for the British Press Awards.) By 30 April, this side of the *Sun*'s activities had expanded further:

> Are you feeling shirty with the enemy? Want to give those damn Argies a whole lot of bargie?
>
> Course you do! Well, here's your chance to put your feelings up front.
>
> Our 'STICK IT UP YOUR JUNTA' T-shirt is a Sunsational reminder of the most popular headline to come out of the Falkland Islands fight.
>
> And it's on offer at the super-low price of only £2. . . .

'THE SUN SAYS KNICKERS TO ARGENTINA!' was the banner headline on 16 April. 'Britain's secret weapon in the Falklands dispute was revealed last night . . . it's undie-cover warfare.' The article revealed that 'thousands of women' were 'sporting specially made underwear embroidered across the front with the proud name of the ship on which a husband or boyfriend is serving.' Even Prince Andrew had 'bought several pairs of battle-briefs. . . . But Palace officials are keeping mum about who will get them as a Royal gift.' Alongside the story was the inevitable picture of 'delightful Debbie Boyland . . . all shipshape and Bristol fashion' in her 'nautical naughties' embroidered with the name of HMS *Invincible*. (It was Tony Snow's report on reaction to this story, dispatched from the carrier three days later, which so aggravated Captain Black.) Within two weeks the *Sun* had returned to the same theme under the headline 'GARTERS TO THE TARTARS', this time with 'Karen Clarke, 19' modelling an *Invincible* garter.

When the *Sun* tackled the actual news of the war it was often wildly wrong. On 7 April the front page was dominated by a picture of a jet airliner and the headline 'OFF TO WAR BY JUMBO!' reporting that four British Airways jumbo jets were to fly '4,000 battle-ready troops to the Ascension Islands [*sic*]'. 'From there', the report went on, 'it is just a seven-hour flight to the occupied islands.' In reality, not only were there no such plans but it would have been physically impossible to use jumbo jets in this way. 'NAVY STORMS SOUTH GEORGIA' was the banner headline days before any attack was mounted. Similarly, also on the front page, on 28 April, the *Sun* proclaimed 'IN WE GO!' Three weeks before the landings the article reported that 'Britain's crack troops were moving in last night for the Battle of the Falklands . . . waiting for the invasion that could be only hours away.'

The 'IN WE GO!' headline came shortly after the start of an eleven-day strike by members of the National Union of Journalists (NUJ) belonging to the *Sun* chapel. The entire paper was being produced by thirteen editorial staff, including MacKenzie and Stephens. 'We hardly got any sleep,' says Stephens. 'We all became totally exhausted. Everyone ate at the office—it was a bit like being in a bunker. Looking back on it, it's amazing that we kept the paper going.' It was in this period that the *Sun* produced some of the best-remembered features of its war coverage, including the 'GOTCHA!' headline, and a story on 1 May which became a *cause célèbre*:

STICK THIS UP YOUR JUNTA!
A Sun missile for Galtieri's gauchos

The first missile to hit Galtieri's gauchos will come with love from the *Sun*.

And just in case he doesn't get the message, the weapon will have painted on the side 'Up Yours, Galtieri' and will be signed by Tony Snow—our man aboard HMS *Invincible*.

The *Sun*—on behalf of all our millions of patriotic readers—has sponsored the missile by paying towards HMS *Invincible*'s victory party once the war is over.

The article was accompanied by a picture of a missile with the caption

'Here it comes, Señors. . . .'

Three days later Tony Snow reported, 'The *Sun* has scored another first . . . by downing an Argentine bomber.' According to Snow, the '*Sun*'s sidewinder' hit one of three Argentine Canberras intercepted by British war planes. He quoted the pilot who carried the *Sun*'s missile: 'Another Harrier and I came up and they did not see us. We got behind them and I fired the missile from fairly close range. A little while later the Canberra blew up.'

The strongest reaction to the missile-sponsoring story came not in London but from the men with the task force. 'A lot of people were very upset,' remembers Gareth Parry. 'There was a general feeling that it was a sick thing to do.' There were letters complaining about it in *Invincible*'s newsletter. Other crewmen complained to Roger Goodwin. On *Canberra* the journalists felt strongly enough to send a joint message to the *Sun* in London. 'Look,' says Peter Stephens, 'we were tired. We just didn't have the time to sit around and have a sage discussion about the rights or wrongs of it.'

Earlier in the crisis, on 10 April, the *Sun* had featured a new video game called 'Obliterate', in which the player commanded a British submarine trying to torpedo Argentine ships. The *Sun* was now presenting the whole war as a video game come to life. First 'with guns blazing a massive Argentinian invasion force grabbed the tiny Falkland Islands in a chilling dawn raid.' Now Britain threatened, in the *Sun*'s words, 'to shoot Argies out of the skies' while 'Navy helicopters blasted two gunboats to smithereens.' The jubilant 'GOTCHA!' which greeted the sinking of the *Belgrano* on 4 May was no aberration. It was the logical culmination of the *Sun*'s coverage. It was the equivalent of ZAP! or POW! or—a headline which the *Sun* actually used later in the war—WALLOP! They were comic-book exclamations used by the *Sun* to describe a fantasy war which bore no resemblance to reality. No other paper, not even the *News of the World* which printed a scorecard:

Britain 6
(South Georgia, two airstrips, three warplanes)
Argentina 0

came as close to portraying the war as a colourful game.

The danger was that the *Sun*, like its counterparts in Argentina with their repeated reports of the sinking of *Invincible*, did nothing to prepare its readers for setbacks. They echoed Mrs Thatcher's famous comment at the outset of the crisis: 'Defeat? The possibility does not exist.' The shock was all the greater, then, when on Tuesday, 4 May, the cowardly, bean-eating, risible gauchos somehow managed to destroy HMS *Sheffield*.

'I shall never forget the horror of the loss of the *Sheffield*,' recalls Stephens. 'It was as though we'd all been kicked in the stomach. There were only thirteen of us. Somehow we had to pick ourselves up off the floor and produce a paper. We had to shovel that story in fast.'

The paper's front page was given over almost entirely to a massive headline: 'BRITISH WARSHIP SUNK BY ARGIES'. Inside, a blank space was substituted for the daily cartoon, dropped 'because it is now considered inappropriate'. In the editorial column the *Sun* reported 'a grievous blow.... YET THIS TRAGEDY, SHOCKING AS IT IS, CAN IN NO WAY AFFECT BRITAIN'S RESOLVE'.

Meanwhile the *Daily Mirror* called the sinking 'Too High a Price':

> Calculating and miscalculating politicians started this conflict. Now it is up to them to end it. Quickly....
>
> Now it is time for the politicians to risk their reputations and find peace. Their biographies should not be written in the blood of others....
>
> It is time to prove that peace through diplomacy is the only policy that pays—and we must do it before there is yet another tragedy at sea.

'The killing has got to stop,' repeated the *Mirror* on 6 May, and produced a startling front page: a long, narrow picture of a grim Mrs Thatcher which ran from top to bottom of the page, with a caption, headline-sized, running down the side of it, a word to a line: 'Outside No 10 where last week she was saying "Rejoice" Mrs Thatcher shows the strain of the desperate days of May.'

Other papers caught the same mood, in particular the *Guardian*, whose cartoonist, Leslie Gibbard, reproduced the famous Donald Zec cartoon of a shipwrecked sailor clinging to a wave-tossed raft, first published in the *Daily Mirror* in 1942. Then the caption had read '"The price of petrol has been increased by one penny"—Official' and had almost led to the *Mirror*'s being closed down under wartime regulations. Now Gibbard changed the caption to read '"The price of *sovereignty* has been increased"—Official.'

Both papers reflected a feeling in the wake of the loss of the

Sheffield that the recovery of the islands might not be worth the sacrifice, that the Royal Navy might be heading for disaster. There was, as will be described below, some panic in Parliament, especially among Conservatives. This found an outlet in attacks upon the BBC, in which Mrs Thatcher joined on 6 May.

The combination of all these events was too much for the *Sun*. A characteristic reaction of ultra-patriotic papers in times of crisis is to turn on 'enemies within'. In the First World War, for example, Horatio Bottomley's *John Bull* attacked Keir Hardie and Ramsay MacDonald, opponents of the war, as 'two traitors within our gates' who should be court-martialled for high treason. The *Sun* lies firmly in the *John Bull* tradition. Critics of the task force before the fleet suffered losses were cowards; sceptics now were traitors. 'Dare call it treason' was the title of the *Sun*'s editorial on Friday, 7 May. Its author was 53-year-old leader writer Ronald Spark, formerly a journalist on the *Daily Express*.

> There are traitors in our midst.
>
> Margaret Thatcher talked about them in the House of Commons yesterday.
>
> She referred to those newspapers and commentators on radio and TV who are not properly conveying Britain's case over the Falklands, and who are treating this country as if she and the Argentines had an equal claim to justice, consideration and loyalty.
>
> The Prime Minister did not speak of treason. The *Sun* does not hesitate to use the word. . . .
>
> What is it but treason to talk on TV, as Peter Snow talked, questioning whether the Government's version of the sea battles was to be believed?
>
> We are caught up in a shooting war, not a game of croquet. There are no neutral referees above the sound of the guns. A British citizen is either on his country's side—or he is its enemy.
>
> What is it but treason for the *Guardian* to print a cartoon, showing a British seaman clinging to a raft, above the caption: '"The price of sovereignty has been increased"—official'?
>
> Isn't that exactly calculated to weaken Britain's resolve at a time when lives have been lost, whatever the justice of her cause?
>
> Imagine a cartoonist who produced a drawing like that in Buenos Aires. Before he could mutter: 'Forgive me, Señors' he would be put up in front of a wall and shot.

The *Guardian*, with its pigmy circulation and absurd posturing, is perhaps not worth attention.

The *Daily Mirror*, however, has pretensions as a mass-sale newspaper.

What is it but treason for this timorous, whining publication to plead day after day for appeasing the Argentine dictators because they do not believe the British people have the stomach for a fight, and are instead prepared to trade peace for honour?

We are truly sorry for the *Daily Mirror*'s readers.

They are buying a newspaper which again and again demonstrates it has no faith in its country and no respect for her people.

'Kelvin felt very strongly,' explains Peter Stephens, who chaired the editorial conference at which the leader was agreed. 'I personally thought "treachery" was a bit too much when applied to individuals.'

Reaction was instantaneous. Ken Ashton, the general secretary of the National Union of Journalists, issued a statement calling it 'odious and hysterical'. To Peter Preston, editor of the *Guardian*, it was 'sad and despicable'. Michael English, a Labour MP, urged the Attorney General to prosecute the *Sun* for criminal libel. The strongest reaction came from the *Daily Mirror*.

When Mike Molloy saw the *Sun* on Friday morning his first instinct was to speak to the paper's legal department, which advised him that the *Mirror* could almost certainly win an action for libel. Instead, he decided to publish a reply. The *Mirror*'s leader writer is Joe Haines, a former press secretary to Harold Wilson. That Friday happened to be his day off, but Molloy called him at home and asked him to come in. The two men discussed the subject briefly. Haines retired to his office, inserted a sheet of paper into his typewriter, and started work. The resulting article took him exactly one hour and ten minutes: 'They're best written that way, when you're angry.' Molloy substituted the word 'harlot' for 'whore' and deleted three lines. ('I can't remember what they were,' says Haines. 'I think they were about Nazi Germany.') Otherwise the editorial ran exactly as Haines had written it, taking up an entire page, illustrated with *Sun* headlines, and captioned 'THE HARLOT OF FLEET STREET'. 'A coarse and demented newspaper' was the *Mirror*'s description of its rival.

There have been lying newspapers before. But in the past month it has broken all records.

It has long been a tawdry newspaper. But since the Falklands crisis began it has fallen from the gutter to the sewer. . . .

It has been seen on American TV as an example of how British newspapers cover the crisis. Far from helping our cause, it shames it.

From behind the safety of its typewriters it has called for battle to commence to satisfy its bloodlust. The *Sun* today is to journalism what Dr Josef Goebbels was to truth. Even *Pravda* would blush to be bracketed with it.

The *Daily Mirror* does not believe that patriotism has to be proved in blood. Especially someone else's blood. . . .

We do not want to report that brave men have died so that the *Sun*'s circulation might flourish.

Though such is the temper of the British people that they are as likely to be repelled by the *Sun*'s treatment of the fighting as is every decent British journalist. . . .

A Labour MP yesterday called for the *Sun* to be prosecuted for criminal libel. There is no point in that. It has the perfect defence: Guilty but insane.

What would be more useful would be if the *Sun* was compelled to carry an official Government announcement on each copy: 'Warning: reading this newspaper may damage your mind.'

Reactions to the *Mirror*'s attack varied. Haines was inundated with letters and phone calls of congratulation, mainly from other journalists, including the leader writer of the *Daily Star*. Michael Foot (who himself later condemned the 'hysterical bloodlust' of the *Sun* in the House of Commons) wrote to Molloy praising the article. So, too, did Lord Cudlipp, the editor who took the *Daily Mirror* to its peak circulation of over 5 million in the 1960s. Some, though, thought it too violent and detected behind it the *Mirror*'s years of frustration at being unable to recapture its old position as Britain's largest-selling daily paper. 'The spectacle of the *Sun* and the *Mirror* at each other's throats has not been a pleasant one,' wrote the advertising trade newspaper *Campaign* on 13 May:

It was absurd of the *Sun* to make its accusations of treason; but it was certainly undignified of the *Mirror*, which until then had been pursuing a moderate line with admirable objectivity, to respond with a full page and a headline shrieking about 'The harlot of Fleet Street'.

'It was hysterical, silly and misguided to give so much space to criticism,' says Peter Stephens. 'A foolish piece of journalism, ludicrously overstated.'

The *Sun* itself claimed, 'Hundreds of readers have phoned us, firmly supporting our views.... True Brit John Platt—a boiler attendant who was in the Navy in World War Two—wept with emotion as he called in to support our condemnation of traitors....' Disarmingly entitled 'Why all the fuss?' the *Sun*'s editorial presented the issue as a threat to press freedom:

> Our message to Mr English, the National Union of Journalists and anyone else who is interested is this:
> We shall not be gagged on any matter of deep public interest.
> We shall treat crude threats with the contempt they deserve.
> As for the BBC, the *Guardian* and the *Daily Mirror* (whose editorial line is now endorsed by the Communist *Morning Star*), we know they are happy when they are dishing it out.
> It remains to be seen whether they can take it.

The following Wednesday, 12 May, the *Sun*'s NUJ chapel met to consider a motion condemning Kelvin MacKenzie for publishing the 'treason' editorial. It was defeated. The views expressed in the *Sun*, claimed the reporters, 'have never been necessarily those of all or even part of the journalists on the newspaper'. Ronald Spark, author of 'Dare call it treason', remained unrepentant. A move to expel him from the NUJ for breaches of the union's code of conduct led to a disciplinary hearing which Spark refused to attend. 'You ask if your committee's session will be convenient for me,' he wrote to the NUJ's Assistant Secretary.

> As far as I am concerned you can meet at midnight on a raft in the middle of the Thames or at any other time or in any other place. I have not the slightest intention of attending, and no one will have any authority to represent me. I shall correspond with you no further. I shall ignore any so-called findings. Had I the common touch of, say, a *Guardian* leader writer, my attitude to your committee could be summed up in two words. Get stuffed.
> Yours truly,
> Ronald Spark

(Spark was finally expelled six months later for a leader described by the NUJ as 'vituperative, callous and clearly designed to inflame public opinion' and which cited 'the law of treason as a weapon with which to prevent others from exercising their rights of free speech'. The NUJ's decision was widely attacked in Fleet Street as an over-reaction, and after an appeal Spark was reinstated.)

For its part, the *Sun* used the publicity to identify itself even more closely with the task force. From 11 May every front page bore the slogan 'THE PAPER THAT SUPPORTS OUR BOYS'. A 'Task Force Action Line' was established, down which the *Sun* poured everything from chocolate biscuits to love poems, from page three pictures to cassettes of the Cup Final, presided over by reporter Muriel Burden, 'Darling of the Fleet'. The comic-strip headlines continued. ARGY JETS SHOT DOWN (13 May), OUR PLANES BLITZ ARGY SHIPS, HOW OUR TOUGH GUYS HIT PEBBLE ISLAND (17 May), ARGIES BLOWN OUT OF THE SKY (24 May), PANICKY ARGIES FLEE BAREFOOT (3 June), HERO BAYONET TROOPS KILL FIFTY (14 June). Following their peace initiative, the 'contemptible, treacherous Irish' joined the *Sun*'s gallery of hate-figures: 'Don't buy Irish golden butter. . . . Don't holiday there this summer. It's not much but it's better than giving succour to our new enemy.' The names of all thirty-three Labour MPs who voted against the Government on 20 May were printed as a 'Roll of Shame'. 'Enemy quail at the touch of cold steel,' reported the *Sun* on 14 June. 'The Argies had no stomach for close-quarters combat and crumbled before the Task Force's full-blooded assaults.' The level of abuse was kept up to the end, even spilling over on to the sports pages during the coverage of the World Cup. 'ARGIES SMASHED. . . . They strutted, they cheated and afterwards they bleated. That was the arrogant Argentines last night. They swaggered on as world champions, and crawled off, humiliated by little Belgium. . . .'

Yet if the *Sun* hoped by such coverage to improve circulation, there was no evidence of that by the end of the war. Throughout the country as a whole there was only a tiny rise in the total circulation of all Fleet Street papers: from 14.9 million per day in March to 15.2 million in May (when fighting was at its height), falling back to 15 million in June—an overall increase of less than 1 per cent. In the same period, the *Sun* actually *lost* sales of 40,000 a day, while the *Mirror* added 95,000. 'We put on 100,000 thanks to a promotional campaign just before the war started,' says Molloy, 'and we managed to keep most of them.' Peter Stephens agrees: 'I don't think anyone prospered or suffered as a result of the war.'

Bearing in mind the precedent of Suez, this was, from the *Mirror*'s point of view, an impressive performance. Why was this? The Falklands war was, after all, a much more popular venture than Suez. If papers opposed to military action lost readers in 1956, surely they should have done even worse in 1982?

In advance of detailed academic research one can only speculate, but it seems almost certain that the explanation lies in the expansion of television over the past twenty-five years. At the time of Suez there were less than 6 million television licence holders in the United Kingdom; today there are around 18 million. By 1971, a BBC Audience Research Unit report found that 86 per cent of the population found television a 'trustworthy' source of news; only 30 per cent 'trusted' newspapers.

The Falklands crisis rammed home the lesson of how powerful a means of communication television has become. When the Ministry of Defence spokesman appeared 'live' on television to announce the latest news from the South Atlantic, the night editor in Fleet Street was receiving the information no more swiftly and in no different a manner from his readers sitting at home. Voice reports from the television correspondents with the task force were arrriving back hours, sometimes days, ahead of written dispatches. Throughout the war, as the *Daily Mail* pointed out in its evidence to the Commons Defence Committee, ·'most of Britain's national newspapers were largely dependent on taking notes from Brian Hanrahan and Michael Nicholson.'

Given this immediacy, fewer people care any more what the *Sun* or the *Mirror* says. With bingo, the mass-circulation papers of Fleet Street are ceasing to be 'newspapers' in the traditional sense. As bingo can apparently lead half a million readers to change their newspaper in a matter of weeks, it is scarcely surprising that the editorial pages are fast turning into wrapping paper for that day's lucky numbers. Add to this the fact that in recent weeks the *Sun* has sometimes had seven pages of sport and a further five of advertising in a twenty-eight-page paper, and the reason why the Falklands war hardly touched circulation may well stand explained.

4. Nott the Nine o'Clock News

The Falklands campaign came to be called 'the worst reported war since the Crimea'. Newspaper correspondents' dispatches from the task force often arrived in London too late to be used; some never arrived at all. The first still picture from the South Atlantic did not come through until 18 May, over three weeks late, and even then it turned out to be an embarrassingly naked propagandist photograph of the Union Jack being unfurled over South Georgia. Newspapers were forced to rely on artists' impressions of what was happening. Pen-and-ink illustrators were called out of retirement. A vigorous, heroic depiction of fighting, normally confined to the pages of *Victor*, found its way on to the news stands and added to the unreality of the war.

For television the situation was on occasion, marginally *worse* than it had been during the Crimea. In 1854 the Charge of the Light Brigade was graphically described in *The Times* twenty days after it took place. In 1982 some TV film took as long as twenty-three days to get back to London, and the average delay for the whole war, from filming to transmission, was seventeen days. 'They almost became the Dead Sea scrolls by the time we got them in,' complained David Nicholas, the editor of ITN. For most of the war, television had to rely for news from the task force on voice reports alone, illustrated by a caption showing a picture of the correspondent who was speaking.

For many broadcasters this 'radiovision' was hard to accept. During the 1960s and 1970s, news reporting changed out of all recognition; nowhere was this revolution greater than in the coverage of wars. From Vietnam onwards, through the struggles in Africa, the Middle East and latterly El Salvador, television has depicted the violence of war from the heart of the fighting. Lightweight, hand-held cameras first enabled television to get to the front line; now electronic newsgathering (ENG) equipment has ensured that such pictures can be transmitted via satellite and studio into millions of homes in the space of a couple of hours. Television gives everyone a ringside seat. In May 1980 British viewers were able to watch the SAS storming the Iranian Embassy as if it were a Cup Final: live, with commentary, at peak time, simultaneously on both main channels. The implications of this access were widely expected to be profound in the event of any future British conflict. Yet for the bulk of the Falklands war, the camera might as well not have been invented. The crisis lasted for seventy-four days, and for the first fifty-four there were no British pictures of any action.

The reason for the lack of pictures was primarily a technical one. Transmitting TV pictures via satellite from on board a fast-moving warship is a vastly more difficult process than transmission from on land. Both the BBC and ITN have their own satellite ground stations, but there was no way in which these could have been properly stabilized to transmit from the deck of a ship; nor did they have the sophisticated auto-tracking equipment necessary to keep the ground station pointing along the critical narrow path of the satellite as the ship changed course. This meant that any pictures transmitted from the task force would have to be sent through the Navy's own satellite communications. The BBC and ITN did everything they could to prize such facilities out of the Ministry of Defence. At a meeting before the aircraft carriers left Portsmouth, Ian McDonald was persuaded to allow an ITN engineer, Peter Heaps, to sail on board *Hermes* and to test her SCOT military satellite terminals to see whether they could be used to broadcast television pictures. The technical problems posed were immense. Television pictures require at least 1,000 times the frequency range used by the normal voice and signal traffic which military satellites are designed to handle.

Nevertheless, according to David Nicholas, things at first looked 'pretty promising'. On 8 April, the BBC and ITN—who acted in concert throughout—had further talks with McDonald, and on 11 April two television engineers were given access to an operational satellite earth station at the Royal Air Force base at Oakhanger. Equipment was modified by ITN and flown out to *Hermes*. But when the ship reached Ascension, Heaps was ordered home by ITN. Nicholas claimed:

> We were told at that stage that in order to get the pictures back we would have to use the SCOT satellite. . . . It was explained to us that in order to do that they would have to close down the

satellite as far as military traffic was concerned for some twenty minutes or half an hour, and they did not wish to do that. . . . That is when we pulled the engineer out. We later learned that there were moments, for one reason and another, and certain phases of the day when the SCOT satellite was closed down anyway. . . . That is something we were never able to establish.

'After this,' wrote the BBC in its evidence to the Commons Defence Committee, 'no real progress was made' until, on 14 May, a technical conference was held at the Royal Signals and Radar Establishment, Defford. Two possible solutions to the impasse were discussed. One was to use the British military satellite SKYNET II, the other to use the American military satellite DISCUS. Extensive tests using simulated transmissions were carried out at Defford on 19 May. To the engineers' delight, black-and-white pictures of reasonable quality were produced; a cassette of the results was shown to the Ministry of Defence.

But once again there were problems. The SKYNET satellite was not in the right position to pick up signals from the task force's area of operations. In order to send pictures back one ship would have had to detach herself from the carrier group and sail to the South Georgia region, which lay just within the area covered by SKYNET. This option was ruled out, leaving the American DISCUS which, according to the BBC's Assistant Director-General, Alan Protheroe, posed even more difficulties:

> to have used the DISCUS satellite would have meant asking the Americans to tilt that satellite very slightly so that its reflection would cover the area which we required. The three American television networks made an approach to the Pentagon to discover what the possibilities were of that satellite being tilted. They were not rejected, if I can put it that way. The request, the suggestion, was not rejected out of hand. The Pentagon, I understand, made it clear that they would require a formal approach from the Ministry of Defence or the British Government. I have no knowledge that such a request was made.

The MoD later admitted that indeed no such formal request *was* made. Instead an 'informal' approach was made at 'desk [*i.e. low*] level'. According to Commander P. H. Longhurst, an MoD communications expert, the response was 'very negative'.

Without satellite facilities, film from the task force simply had to be put on the next ship heading back to Ascension. In an age of supposedly instant communications, what were perhaps the most eagerly awaited television pictures in the world travelled homewards at a steady 25 knots. Other ingenious solutions, such as attaching cassettes of ENG material to balloons and allowing them to drift until picked up by a Nimrod aircraft, were discussed in a desultory way, and dismissed.

Although ITN and the BBC later went out of their way to pay tribute to the enthusiasm of individual officers, there was a general feeling among the broadcasters that the MoD was not particularly anxious to ensure a regular flow of television pictures. ITN was 'convinced that satellite pictures could have been transmitted from *Hermes*. But there was an absence of will by high authority to try it.' Alan Protheroe also spoke of a 'lack of will': 'A crusty RN officer said to me: "You're the chappie who wanted to put that satellite thing in the middle of the flight deck. Would've stopped us flying, y'know...." There are moments when a long, slow pull at a stiff Scotch is the only possible response.'

Although the MoD is insistent that the lack of pictures was solely due to technical problems, other evidence suggests that the broadcasters' suspicions may have some foundation. Ministers, military chiefs and civil servants freely admit in private their relief that there were no television pictures to worry about. Sir Frank Cooper said in July:

> To be quite frank about it, if we had had transmission of television throughout, the problems of what could or could not be released would have been very severe indeed. We have been criticized in many quarters, and we will no doubt go on being criticized in many quarters, but the criticism we have had is a small drop in the ocean compared to the problems we would have had in dealing with the television coverage.

With 'very severe' problems envisaged in the higher reaches of the Government, it is scarcely surprising that the broadcasters detected a 'lack of will' when it came to facilitating regular television coverage. Sir Frank Cooper was airing a general anxiety, known to have been shared by, among others, John Nott.

When the collected coverage of the campaign *was* eventually broadcast, after the Argentine surrender, it included some harrowing shots of badly burned faces and blown-off limbs. But the worst material was never shown. It was weeded out by the television companies themselves. Major-General Sir Jeremy Moore, the commander of the British land forces, afterwards wanted 'to pay tribute to the good taste of our journalists that they did not show anything as unpleasant as could have been available'. Imagine the nightmare which would have faced the Ministry of Defence in London if pictures of air attacks and casualties, of men suffering from strain and fear, had been coming back every day at the height of the fighting. What pictures would have been censored? And on what grounds? As Neville Taylor, the present chief of public relations at the MoD, later put it:

> I know a lot of film was taken which they [the TV editors] decided . . . was of such a nature that they did not wish to put it on the screen. Had there been live television, I do not think one can simply say, 'Well, of course, it would be censored.' We would be entering into the realms of style and content and taste, *which I am sure we have got to do* [author's emphasis], but at the moment I cannot see a way of establishing criteria that establish that deletion of that film clip is OK and that bit is all right, if one is talking about sensitivities on taste and not operational security.

The Ministry would have been caught in a political minefield. Too much censorship and there would have been accusations that the Government was attempting to 'sanitize' the war; too little and there would have been outrage from the military and from distressed relatives.

Even with the trickle of pictures that did come back there were problems. Whenever material from the task force arrived at the BBC, the MoD was immediately informed, and senior army and naval officers would hasten to Television Centre in west London for a viewing. But, complained the BBC, the officers 'appeared not to be fully briefed and differed in their attitudes to their task'. Enraged editors found censorship going far beyond security and straying into questions of 'taste' and 'tone'. The BBC was told not to use a picture of a body in a bag, not to use the phrase 'horribly burned', not to show a pilot confessing, jokingly, that he had been 'scared fartless' on one mission. 'Clearance', rather than emotive words like 'censorship' or 'vetting', was the Ministry's euphemism for this extraordinary process.

In the face of unacceptable material, the bureaucrats always had their traditional stand-by: procrastination. Two voice dispatches (without pictures) came in simultaneously describing the disaster at Bluff Cove in which fifty British servicemen were killed. Michael Nicholson's was 'up-beat', speaking of 'a day of extraordinary heroism'. Brian Hanrahan's was more sombre, talking of a 'setback' for the British and including a line which the censors in London found offensive: 'Other survivors came off unhurt but badly shaken after hearing the cries of men trapped below.' Nicholson's piece was passed. Hanrahan's was temporarily blocked. By the time it was released, with the distasteful line cut, the news bulletins were over and both ITN and the BBC had been forced to use the Nicholson version.

Similarly, when film material reached Ascension after its long sea voyage from the Falklands, or even when it finally arrived in Britain, it was, according to the BBC, often 'deliberately delayed'. Several consignments were considered sensitive and were held up, without further explanation, for 'security reasons'. Small wonder that the BBC's evidence to MPs after the war was unusually uncompromising and outspoken: 'In this area it is the BBC's deep concern that the Ministry of Defence has come very close to the "management" or "manipulation" of news, an idea that is alien to the concept of communication within a free society.' It was not that the broadcasters objected to the argument that some pictures were too shocking to be shown, especially when families of the men concerned might be watching. Indeed, the evidence of what occurred after the war, when the worst pictures were discarded and the military expressed their gratitude, shows that television was ready to censor itself and to abide by the rules of 'good taste'. *The objection was to the Ministry of Defence's deciding how the war would be presented.* The special circumstances of the Falklands campaign ensured that the Government had unique control over how the war appeared on television. Because there were no satellite facilities, the MoD could regulate the flow of pictures and deodorize the war in a way that few other democratic Governments—especially recent Administrations in the USA—have been able to get away with.

The American experience in Vietnam did as much as anything to shape the way in which the British Government handled television during the Falklands crisis. To ITN it seemed that 'the Vietnam analogy was a spectre constantly stalking the Falklands decision-makers and was invoked privately by the military as an object lesson in how not to deal with the media.' To the American-born defence correspondent of the *Economist*, Jim Meacham—who actually served as an officer in Vietnam—civil servants and soldiers often observed: 'This is why you Americans lost the Vietnam war, because you had a free press.' General Moore described how the possibility of 'gory pictures' being shown on TV 'brought forcefully home to me the problem that the Americans had during the Vietnam conflict'. The theme recurs repeatedly in off-the-record conversations with the men who shaped official policy with regard to the handling of the media. As it was clearly such a vital factor in conditioning attitudes, it is perhaps worth considering briefly how valid it is to draw an analogy between the two wars.

On the face of it, they were totally dissimilar. One lasted two and a half months; the other lasted the best part of a decade. One involved a relatively small professional force; the other was fought by hundreds of thousands of conscripts. One was fought on British territory; the other was a war of intervention in a foreign country. One was essentially a maritime expedition; in the other the fighting covered several countries. In virtually every respect the two had nothing in common. One of the few things they did share, however, was that they were both fought in the age of television; and because America's first major military defeat coincided with the advent of TV, there was a tendency, especially among the armed forces, to connect the two. This may be a convenient excuse for the Pentagon. It is scarcely borne out by the facts.

Jim Meacham told the Commons Defence Committee:

> I speak as a person who fought as a serving officer of medium grade, so I suppose I bore some responsibility for the loss of the war. We lost because we fought it wrong, not because the free press reported it right. I do not accept this for a minute. At the end of the day the American public and the American Congress forced the Administration to give up this war because it was not going to win. The body politic does not have any sharp instruments; it has only blunt-edged instruments. The Government had five years with almost unlimited expenditure to

fight this war and failed to win it and I think gradually the body politic, the electorate, Congress, came to realize it was not going to win. Through the medium of the free press, which had by and large reported the war fairly accurately (although obviously mistakes were made), the American public got a picture of that war and ended it. If there is an argument for a free press in a democratic country, this surely is it, that imperfectly they did come to the conclusion that they had to end this war and did end it.

If you work from the assumption that the Vietnam war was something worth going on with, that the Americans could have won it, that it would have been better had they stayed, anything that worked against that, including television, was harmful. Television showed the brutality of what was a particularly bloody war, and it emphasized, by the constant repetition of pictures each night, how long it was dragging on and how little was being achieved. If, on the other hand, you work from the assumption—as most Americans now do—that the Vietnam war was a mistake in the first place, how can you blame television? The reverses were purely military ones. The costs, human and economic, proved too great to be borne. Television merely reflected this state of affairs. It did not create it. The Tet offensive was mounted by the Vietcong, not CBS. To reason that because Vietnam was televised and was also lost, *ipso facto* any war extensively televised can never be won is a logical absurdity.

Nor is it true to say that exposure to television pictures of blood and gore prompted people to become more pacific. American viewers saw vastly more horrific images of war than did British viewers of the Falklands conflict. They saw, to pick merely the most famous examples, a man being executed by being shot in the head, a girl plastered with burning nepalm, and Morley Safer's 1965 film of American soldiers methodically destroying the village of Cam Ne. Yet evidence suggests that prolonged TV coverage actually encouraged the American public to *support* the war. A survey conducted by *Newsweek* in 1967 found that 64 per cent of viewers felt *more* like 'backing up the boys in Vietnam' as a result of watching TV; only 26 per cent said it made them feel more hostile to the war. By 1972 a further *Newsweek* survey revealed that people were becoming progressively more indifferent to the horrors being repeated nightly on their TV screens. The war had become unreal. Television, wrote

Michael J. Arlen, the TV critic of the *New Yorker*, 'for all the industry's advances, still shows one a picture of men three inches tall shooting at other men three inches tall'. As Philip Knightley later put it in his book on war correspondents, *The First Casualty*: 'when seen on a small screen, in the enveloping and cosy atmosphere of the household, some time between the afternoon soap-box drama and the late-night war movie, the television version of the war in Vietnam could appear as just another drama.' A prominent American psychiatrist, Fredric Wertham, found that TV had the effect of conditioning viewers to accept war. Some might argue that this dulling of the senses and confusion of reality with fantasy is potentially much more dangerous than any sapping of the appetite for war by nightly exposure to its agonies.

The MoD, naturally, did not see it that way. As early as 1970, at a Royal United Services Institute seminar, the then Director of Defence Operations, Plans and Supplies at the Ministry of Defence, Brigadier F. G. Caldwell, told his audience that after Vietnam, if Britain were to go to war again, 'we would have to start saying to ourselves, are we going to let television cameras loose on the battlefield?'

Twelve years later, the evidence of the military commanders in the Falklands to the House of Commons Defence Committee shows how much the Caldwell interpretation of Vietnam still held sway. 'Thank heavens we did not have unpleasant scenes shown,' said Brigadier Tony Wilson, the commanding officer of 5 Brigade. 'It would have been singularly debilitating to our wives and our families.' Wilson, Moore, Captains Black and Middleton and the task force commander, Admiral Woodward, all believed that their men would have preferred their families at home not to see precisely what they were involved in. To Wilson it was a 'merciful relief' that between the landing on the Falklands and the ceasefire 'we got no letters, therefore we were totally unaware of the effect that the war was having on our own wives and the like.' General Moore spoke of the 'very great strain' felt by his 11-year-old son 'because he was very conscious that our pictures were on radio and television every day. ... he felt a very heavy responsibility, almost as if he was commanding the land forces, poor chap.'

There is a great danger here that subjective reasons, like General Moore's understandable concern about his son, based on a partial view of the American experience in Vietnam, may combine to prevent television coverage of war on the dubious grounds of its possible effects on morale rather than for clearly understood reasons of operational security. The military are always going to insist on the maximum amount of secrecy: 'I wouldn't tell the people anything until the war is over,' an American military censor is reported to have remarked, 'and then I'd tell them who won.' But if we allow censors to stray from straightforward matters of security and enter into questions of taste and tone and 'national morale', we are in a different area. In a war in which the homeland is threatened with invasion and the whole of the native system of government is at stake, clearly the morale of the ordinary citizen is a vital consideration. In such circumstances some freedoms may have temporarily to be suspended, as they were in the Second World War. But in relatively limited operations like the Falklands, can the same criteria be applied? Is it legitimate for the Government to deny its people the right to see such things as bodies in bags or to hear phrases such as 'horribly burned'?

The Falklands war went on long enough to raise such questions, but not long enough to answer them. A few more weeks' fighting, a few more television pictures, and we might indeed have learned how far the Government and the military have taken the so-called 'lessons of Vietnam' to heart.

Some idea of the complexity of the relationship between politicians, civil servants, military commanders and television can be seen in the way all four reacted to the first and most shocking of Britain's reverses in the Falklands campaign: the loss of HMS *Sheffield* on 4 May.

Sheffield, a Type 42 destroyer with a crew of 270, was on picket duty 20 miles ahead of the main British carrier group when shortly after 2 p.m. she was hit by a single, air-launched Exocet missile. On board *Hermes* Brian Hanrahan saw 'a pillar of white smoke on the horizon, which continued to climb until dark and the decision was made to abandon her'. Two frigates, *Arrow* and *Yarmouth*, were sent to help fight the fire, but their efforts were in vain and at seven o'clock that evening the ship was finally abandoned.

Confused signals of what had happened began arriving in London towards the end of the afternoon. By 6 p.m. Mrs Thatcher had been told, and an emergency meeting of Ministers and service chiefs was convened at her room in the House of Commons. The mood, according to one of those present, was 'very grim'. Clearly, a statement would have to be issued soon: already, by 7.40, the BBC had heard through 'political sources' that *Sheffield* had been hit and was pressing for further news. Throughout the war, the British were anxious not to give extra credence to Argentine statements by allowing them to be first with the news of British losses. Accordingly, Ian McDonald, the Ministry of Defence's official spokesman and at this point in the war still the official in charge of the MoD's public relations department, hastened to the House of Commons. He waited outside Mrs Thatcher's room until, shortly before 9 p.m., John Nott emerged briefly to tell him that the meeting had agreed to announce the attack on *Sheffield*. McDonald raced back to the MoD Press Centre, set up two days before and housed in one of the MoD's large 'historic' rooms. He is said to have drafted the details of the short statement on the journey back from Parliament.

The BBC's main television bulletin, the *Nine o'Clock News* was actually on the air when McDonald burst into the Press Centre. The BBC's political editor, John Cole, was talking about the day's events at Westminster. He was suddenly told through his earpiece to wind up his report, and the BBC switched through live to the MoD. McDonald, seated like a newsreader behind a desk, was given a cue by the BBC cameraman and began to read.

> In the course of its duties within the total exclusion zone around the Falkland Islands, HMS *Sheffield*, a Type 42 destroyer, was attacked and hit late this afternoon by an Argentine missile. The ship caught fire which spread out of control.
>
> When there was no longer any hope of saving the ship, the ship's company abandoned ship.
>
> All who abandoned her were picked up. It is feared there have been a number of casualties, but we have no details of them yet.
>
> Next of kin will be informed first as soon as details are received.

McDonald was so nervous during the reading of this statement that at one point he thought he would never be able to reach the end.

For anyone who saw it, it was a dramatic piece of television: the news bulletin proceeding in its usual way, a momentary confusion, and then the dramatic appearance of the sombre, dark-suited McDonald with his funereal parody of an announcer's voice. It was a shock deeply resented by many of the professional broadcasters, who had no opportunity to soften its impact and who felt they were being forced into a position of treating McDonald almost as if he were one of their own correspondents. Richard Francis, a former director of News and Current Affairs at the BBC, spoke of McDonald's 'eerie style' as he delivered the news 'in a way that hit at the stomachs of the country'. There were 12 million viewers of the *Nine o'Clock News* that night, the largest audience reached by the programme in the whole course of the war. 'We had no opportunity to condition this mass audience to what was to follow,' claimed Francis. The news was heard simultaneously all over the country: by wives and families of men who had been on board *Sheffield*, by fellow naval officers in the wardroom at Devonport, where McDonald's statement was greeted by a stunned silence followed by swearwords, and by MPs at the Palace of Westminster.

The House of Commons is the kind of institution that is easily swept by panic and rumour. John Nott had already told the Leader of the House, John Biffen, that he was not prepared to make a statement that night, but now the Conservative Whips began to come under intense pressure from nervous back-benchers. In the Chamber, a debate on Scottish local government was in progress when the news broke. MPs of all parties rose one after the other to demand a statement on the loss of the *Sheffield*, and finally, much against his will, Nott came in to the Chamber a few moments before 11 p.m. Some indication of the confusion within the Ministry of Defence can be gathered from the fact that Nott began by saying that twelve men were missing, and a few minutes later a note was seen being passed along the benches from his Civil Service advisors forcing him to revise his estimate of casualties in the light of fresh news to thirty.

While all this was going on in London, 8,000 miles away Brian Hanrahan and Michael Nicholson were filming survivors coming on board *Hermes*. By listening to conversations on the bridge, by talking to men rescued from *Sheffield* and from snippets of information picked up from friendly officers, the two men had arrived at a 'rough order of magnitude' of casualties, which led them to believe, said Hanrahan, that it was 'something below fifty'. 'Certainly by six o'clock in the evening', claimed Nicholson, 'we knew that most of the survivors had been rescued, that *Sheffield* was still afloat.' But to Nicholson's chagrin, he was prevented from sending a dispatch stating, '*Sheffield* has been hit. She is still afloat. Most of the crew has been saved.' Nor was Bernard Hesketh, the TV cameraman, allowed to hitch a lift in one of the helicopters travelling between the carriers and *Sheffield* to film what was happening. 'There were a lot of people to get to and fro,' explained Admiral Woodward later, 'fire-fighting equipment and all the rest, so on the afternoon of the strike there was no question of getting press there, and the premium on weight per helicopter was a matter of lifesaving, not of photographing chaps drowning.'

A day of frustration for the reporters was capped when the BBC World Service, picked up on board ship, broadcast McDonald's statement, and later reported Nott as telling the House of Commons that *Sheffield* had been sunk and it was not known how many survivors there were. Later Nicholson supplied the Commons Defence Committee with a bowdlerized version of his diary entry for 4 May. The full entry was more outspoken:

> Action stations piped 1310 hours, enemy planes detected on 118 degrees: 1420 hours HMS *Sheffield* hit by single Exocet from Etendard fired from six miles. Survivors came aboard. RAF Vulcan bomber makes 2nd attack on Stanley airfield . . . also our Harriers have another go. One of our planes is missing . . . Nick Taylor's. We are not allowed to report any of this. *I stick my neck out all day on this island sweating every time I hear a red air alert and at the end of the day I hear some fart who goes to bed every night in London* [i.e. McDonald announcing the news]. We are suffering heroic redundancy.

The frustrations continued throughout the days which followed. On 5 May, the day after the attack on *Sheffield*, her captain, Sam Salt, and some of his men, were found by Nicholson 'in the dark on the floor of the hangar deck'. 'Extraordinary man,' noted Nicholson. 'Agrees to be interviewed but MoD PR intervenes and Salt is taken away for a briefing. He returns two hours later, a different and much-subdued man.' It was Nicholson's belief that Salt 'had been told about certain areas he should not talk about and was a totally different man . . . they were censoring before the camera was switched on.'

Another incident which suggests that the Navy was concerned with censoring as much on the grounds of taste and tone as on strictly military criteria occurred two days later, when the body of a *Sheffield* casualty was buried at sea from the quarter-deck of *Hermes*. The television reporters were told to keep away: 'It wouldn't be decent to film it.' In a later argument with the MoD minder on *Hermes*,

Graham Hammond, Nicholson recorded Hammond as telling him: 'You must have been told you couldn't report bad news before you left. You knew when you came you were expected to do a 1940 propaganda job.'

The Navy naturally did not want bad publicity—and as it controlled every facet of the environment in which the journalists worked, it was well placed to get its own way. For several days after the attack on *Sheffield* repeated requests to be allowed to send Bernard Hesketh to film the still-burning ship were refused. 'We were interested in hiding the fact that *Sheffield* was still afloat from the Argentinians,' says Woodward, 'because that might have encouraged them to attack again.' This seems an odd excuse, given the fact that there was no way the television pictures (which would anyway be subject to censorship) could be got back quickly to London. Eventually, after three days, Woodward relented—but only because he needed the pictures for his own use. 'It became necessary for me to have rather more direct information, if I could, of the state of the ship.' Hesketh was accordingly sent off in a helicopter and flew over the burning hulk. The Admiral was pleased with the result: 'They took some jolly good photographs which were of immense use to me.' Only after the cassette of ENG material had been fully analysed on a video machine by Woodward and his advisors was it released to the broadcasters. The following day HMS *Sheffield* sank.

The announcement of *Sheffield*'s sinking, when it was made back in London, revealed another way in which the authorities subtly 'cleaned up' the image of the war for television. Sir Henry Leach, the First Sea Lord, instructed Ian McDonald not to announce the final loss of *Sheffield* in a televised statement. 'The discreet black and white of newsprint was considered more dignified than the glare of television,' was how one insider described the reasoning behind this decision. Each day McDonald would read a statement to the media. He would then pause, order the cameras and lights to be switched off, and then answer questions. Television was allowed to record only the statement, never the question-and-answer sessions. It was in one of these non-televised exchanges that McDonald let slip the fact that *Sheffield* had sunk. (The refusal to allow after the statement, the televising of any further comments—which were attributable and not off the record—was justified on the grounds that a 'code' had sprung up between McDonald and the press, in which he would hedge, fence and often joke, behaviour which was considered likely to 'confuse' a mass audience and which would have robbed McDonald of his aura of omnipotence.)

When the public did finally see the television pictures of the events surrounding the loss of *Sheffield*, they were three weeks old. The pictures of the survivors and the interview with Captain Salt were filmed on 4 and 5 May and transmitted on the night of 26 May. The pictures of *Sheffield* taken for Admiral Woodward on 7 May were finally shown in London on 28 May. By then the landings had taken place at San Carlos Bay, fighting on the Falklands had been going on for a week, and the war had moved into a completely different phase.

Television's presentation of the loss of *Sheffield* showed the extent of the authorities' control over the media: the terse official statement in London, the restrictions on filming and reporting imposed by the Navy, the use of non-televised question-and-answer sessions to minimize the impact of bad news, the painfully slow progress home of pictures, so that they were of little more than historical interest by the time they arrived. 'There has been confusion,' insisted the BBC at the end of the war. 'There have been failures. . . . Above all, there has been a failure of perception of the role of the media in a free society at a time of conflict. Even within the identifiable parameters of security, there have been attempts to "manage" or "manipulate" the news.' Subsequently questioned about these allegations by the Labour MP·John Gilbert, Sir Frank Cooper was unrepentant:

> We did not produce the full truth and the full story and you, as a politician, know as well as anyone else that on many occasions the news is handled by everybody in politics in a way which rebounds to their advantage. I regard that as something for politicians to decide but where lives are at stake, as they were in this case, I believe it was right to do as we did and I have never lost a moment's sleep on it.

Television journalists, like newspaper reporters, expect that in the normal course of events politicians and civil servants will try to manipulate them. But the situation during the Falklands crisis was not normal. The unique circumstances of the campaign gave the authorities virtually complete control over news of the fighting. Information, especially pictures, came out in a thin trickle.

This had some exotic side-effects. Current affairs programmes came to resemble a strange hybrid between children's television and sport. Tasteful watercolours had to represent what was happening in two of the areas to which cameras had no access: Parliament and the South Atlantic. Toy models of ships and aircraft moved endlessly across giant maps (or 'sandpits' in TV jargon). Around these clustered retired military commanders, passing their professional comments on the match in progress, on likely tactics and possible results. Clips from promotional films for planes, ships and missiles became scratched through repeated showings. . . .

To the increasing annoyance of officials and some politicians, the networks turned for news to Argentina. For the first time in history, television could freely report the enemy's view of the war. There were interviews with ordinary Argentinians and even with military officers. Film of the war taken by Argentine TV was shown in Britain. And, perhaps inevitably, some slight credence began to be given to the Argentine version of events as a result.

> One of the most disturbing elements in the 'information war' [claimed the BBC] was the change in approach of the Argentines. Initially, the Argentine claims were patently hysterical, self-evidently propagandist, and unerringly identified as such by the broadcasters . . . but to our intense dismay, it began to emerge that some of the Argentine claims were possibly true and accurate. Journalists realized (with considerable difficulty, and with alarm, let it be said) that increasingly Argentine claims merited close examination, and should not, as hitherto, be rejected out of hand. The in-built delays in the MoD system, which prevented swift rejection or confirmation of such claims, was a self-inflicted wound. It gave the Argentines, internationally, a credibility they did not deserve. The MoD's information was, too often, the 'runner-up'.
>
> And that, perhaps, was the greatest damage of all.

By the beginning of May, BBC executives in Portland Place and White City were feeling thoroughly frustrated. They had no pictures. They had a strong suspicion that they were being used and that the MoD was not telling them the whole truth. They had programmes to fill and precious little information to go on. For news they were having to rely increasingly on statements from Buenos Aires and leaks from intelligence sources in Washington. . . . The effect on the BBC's coverage began to be noticed, especially within the Conservative Party.

Newsnight was reckoned by the BBC to be having 'a good war'. Its speciality—explaining in detail the background to daily events—was ideally suited to the fast-moving Falklands story. The programme was extended from five to seven nights a week; on some evenings its normal audience was quadrupled. On Sunday, 2 May, the programme's defence expert, Peter Snow, was trying to analyse precisely what was going on in the South Atlantic, using information from Britain, the United States and Argentina. 'Until the British are demonstrated either to be deceiving us or to be concealing losses from us,' he concluded, 'we can only tend to give a lot more credence to their version of events.'

The programme had only just come off the air when a complaint came in from the Conservative MP for Harrow, John Page. *Newsnight*, he said, was 'totally offensive and almost treasonable'. Page's anger was provoked by what he called the BBC's 'unacceptably evenhanded' approach to the war in balancing reports from the MoD against those of Argentina. Page, a 62-year-old former Royal Artillery officer, was not the only angry viewer. In his sixth-floor office in the Ministry of Defence, Frank Cooper—though an old admirer of Snow's—was watching *Newsnight* with increasing exasperation ('Peter was behaving as if he were a disinterested referee,' commented Cooper).

The following day the BBC moved in swiftly to try to quell the beginning of the controversy:

> In times of hostility, as at all other times [ran an official statement], the BBC has to guard its reputation for telling the truth. In its coverage of the situation in the South Atlantic, BBC Television and Radio has reported British, American and Argentine statements and reactions while stressing the unreliability of Argentine claims.

The storm might have blown over. But then, on Tuesday, came the news of the loss of *Sheffield*. A mood close to panic gripped the Conservative Party. 'It was a terrible night,' recalled Julian Critchley, a back-bench Conservative MP. 'For the first time there was a realization that what we had started might end badly—not just for the Tory Party, but for the nation and for everyone involved in the task force.' In this emotional state many Conservative MPs were in no mood to listen to the BBC's Reithian pronouncements about guarding a reputation for truth. Until now the BBC had been reporting the war. From this point on it was part of it.

5. The Enemy Within

The BBC is rarely popular with Prime Ministers, especially Prime Ministers in time of war. As long ago as the Second World War, Winston Churchill, according to Lord Reith, described the Corporation as 'an enemy within the gates, doing more harm than good'.

At the time of the Suez crisis, Anthony Eden was incensed by what he saw as the BBC's unpatriotic behaviour: he found it 'insulting' that the Australian premier, Robert Menzies, was initially denied the opportunity to give a television broadcast in support of the British Government on the grounds that this would be unfair to the Opposition. He was equally furious to discover that BBC World Service programmes were quoting British newspapers antipathetic to his policies over the Canal, and that the Labour leader Hugh Gaitskell was to be given the right of reply to his prime ministerial broadcast. Relations deteriorated to a point at which, in October 1956, the Prime Minister ordered the Lord Chancellor, Lord Kilmuir, 'to prepare an instrument which would take over the BBC altogether and subject it wholly to the will of the Government'. 'The next I heard,' wrote Harman Grisewood, at that time chief assistant to the BBC's Director-General, 'was that Eden had found Kilmuir's draft inadequate and he had been asked to prepare something stronger.' No wonder that on 28 November the writer and broadcaster Harold Nicolson noted: 'The BBC are very fussy about not making any controversial remarks about Suez.' Illness and defeat intervened before Eden could take his schemes any further.

Given this record, it is not surprising that the BBC braced itself for trouble from the outset of the Falklands crisis. The young BBC journalist who produced the Menzies broadcast when it eventually took place after pressure from Eden was Alasdair Milne. Twenty-six years later, he was the BBC's Director-General-designate. 'I always thought the Government would turn on us,' he remarked. 'Once there were losses and the Government came under pressure, they would be likely to turn on the media and the BBC in particular. But it happened several days later than I expected.'

Such an attack was all the more likely given the personality of Mrs Thatcher. Within six months of taking office in 1979 she had attacked the BBC in Parliament and called on it to 'put its own house in order' following some filming of the IRA. Repeated bouts of anger, both privately and publicly expressed, punctuated the following two years. Generally ill at ease on television, Mrs Thatcher is inclined to tick off the media in much the same way as she is said to hector her colleagues.

A good example of this tendency during the Falklands conflict— the memory of which still causes her staff to wince—came after the recapture of South Georgia on 25 April, when she emerged from 10 Downing Street and strode in front of the television cameras with John Nott and a retinue of advisers in tow. 'Ladies and gentlemen, the Secretary of State for Defence has just come over to give me some very good news, and I think you'd like to have it at once.' Mrs Thatcher nodded to Nott. 'The, er, message we've got...,' he began, and went on to read out Admiral Woodward's signal: 'The white ensign flies alongside the Union Jack in South Georgia. God save the Queen.' An immediate chorus of 'What happens next?' arose from the assembled reporters. 'Just rejoice at that news,' instructed the Prime Minister, firmly, 'and congratulate our forces and the marines. Good night, gentlemen.' Mrs Thatcher walked back to No. 10 pursued by questions: 'Are we going to declare war on Argentina?' 'Rejoice!' came the parting injunction from the retreating Prime Minister before the door was slammed, literally in the media's face.

The Prime Minister herself did not see *Newsnight* on 2 May but her advisers did, and when, on 6 May, John Page rose to ask her about the media during Questions to the Prime Minister, she was well prepared. Would she, asked Page, in the course of her 'extremely busy and responsible day',

> try to find a few moments to listen to the radio and watch television, and judge for herself whether she feels that the British case on the Falkland Islands is being presented in a way that is likely to give due confidence to friends overseas and support and encouragement to our Service men and their devoted families?

The Prime Minister replied:

> Judging by many of the comments that I have heard from those
> who watch and listen more than I do, many people are very
> concerned indeed that the case for our British forces is not being
> put over fully and effectively. I understand that there are times
> when it seems that we and the Argentines are being treated
> almost as equals and almost on a neutral basis. I understand that
> there are occasions when some commentators will say that the
> Argentines did something and then 'the British' did something.
> I can only say that if this is so it gives offence and causes great
> emotion among many people.

Other Conservative MPs followed the Prime Minister's lead.
Speaking on the same day to a London conference on terrorism and
the media, Winston Churchill, a Conservative defence spokesman,
attacked broadcasters for 'reporting live propaganda out of Buenos
Aires', and added, without any apparent sense of irony: 'I believe it to
be a travesty of the role of the journalist to swallow hand-outs and
report what is provided at face value. . . . I believe one must exercise
one's judgement and not allow oneself to become a vehicle for
propaganda and misleading information.' Robert Adley, MP for
Christchurch and Lymington, accused the BBC of being 'General
Galtieri's fifth column in Britain. Conservative papers in Fleet Street
joined in. The *Sun* denounced Peter Snow as being among the
'traitors in our midst' (see chapter 3). The *Daily Mail* felt that 'Mrs
Thatcher was quite right when she criticized some of the Falklands
news coverage on radio and television.'

A few hours after the Prime Minister's comments, the BBC's
Chairman, George Howard, had an opportunity to reply in an after-
dinner speech at the Hilton Hotel. The Corporation, he insisted, 'is
not, and could not be, neutral as between our own country and the
aggressor'.

> Coupled with that is a determination that in war, truth shall not
> be the first casualty. . . . The public is very rightly anxious
> about the future, and deserves in this democracy to be given as
> much information as possible. Our reports are believed around
> the world precisely because of our reputation for telling the
> truth.

The BBC did not change its policy. Despite complaints,

newsreaders continued to refer to 'the British' rather than to 'our' forces—a decision based on precedents established in 1939 and reaffirmed in 1956. 'If you start talking about "our troops" and "our ships",' explained Milne, 'then it is natural to speak of "our policy" when you mean the present Government's policy, and then our objectivity would no longer be credible.' This restriction was not applied to the task-force correspondents who came to identify very closely with the men they were with and who spoke of 'we' and 'our'.

On the following Saturday night (8 May) the evening news reported on the funeral of Argentine seamen killed in British attacks, included film of a Buenos Aires press conference, 'and—to add insult to injury—' complained Robert Adley, 'we had a film of the Argentine–Bulgaria football match with a great show of national fervour.' It was the start of a busy period for BBC telephonists as callers rang in to complain about 'disgusting' even-handedness and 'undue reverence' for Argentine casualties. These skirmishes were but a curtain-raiser for the open warfare that was to come.

That weekend, a few hundred yards from Television Centre, in the crumbling old studios in Lime Grove which once housed British Gaumont, *Panorama* finished the first rough assembly of a film about opposition to the war. For more than a week, reporter Michael Cockerell and producer Tim Shawcross had been interviewing opponents of the Government's policy. The rough-cut was viewed by the head of BBC television current affairs programmes, by *Panorama*'s editor, and by the programme's recently arrived presenter, Robert Kee. Kee, in particular, violently disliked the film, and a long list of changes was agreed; twenty alterations were made to the script, and there were a further eighteen cuts in the film itself. One entire sequence, an interview with a dissenting Conservative MP, Robert Hicks, was dropped. Four anti-war voices remained: those of two Labour MPs, George Foulkes and Tam Dalyell, and two Conservatives, David Crouch and Sir Anthony Meyer. Eduardo Crawley, a journalist, analysed the war as it appeared from Buenos Aires. Such a film was likely to be controversial at any time. Following a week in which television's treatment of the war had already been attacked in Parliament by the Prime Minister, the programme was destined from the outset to provoke uproar.

The film was due to be transmitted on Monday 10 May. That morning, a meeting of Mrs Thatcher's inner circle of Ministers, the 'War Cabinet', discussed the whole question of the media and the

Falklands campaign. One of the prime objectives of the Government was to keep public support for the war at a high level, especially following the loss of the *Sheffield*. There was concern at the way in which the war was coming across on television and a considerable amount of criticism of the MoD for the lack of television pictures: the task force had now been at sea for more than five weeks, and still nothing had come back to London. (Significantly, two days later the MoD once more got in touch with the broadcasting organizations to have another try at getting pictures back by satellite.) Fresh from this discussion, the Foreign Secretary, Francis Pym, went straight to a meeting of the House of Commons Foreign Affairs Select Committee. Once again the question of television was raised, this time by yet another Conservative back-bencher, Peter Mills, the MP for Devon West. 'All of us are aware of the criticisms of the presentation, particularly by the BBC,' Pym told the committee. 'The Government are very concerned about it indeed.' He urged anyone in the country who disapproved of the BBC to write to the Corporation direct. It had not been a good day for the broadcasters, and it was by no means over yet.

'Good evening,' began Robert Kee at the start of that night's *Panorama*. 'The Government, the country, perhaps the world itself, is precariously balanced this evening. . . .' The first item in the programme was an interview in New York with Jorge Herera Vegas, the Argentine Minister to the United Nations. After five inconclusive minutes of this, Kee appeared once more in order to present a long and in parts tortuous introduction to Michael Cockerell's film. Instead of labelling it, simply and clearly, as a film about the minority view of the Falklands, Kee devoted about three minutes to a restatement of various points of view, including those of Argentina, Mrs Thatcher and the Archbishop of Canterbury. The fact that what followed was not meant to be a representative report on the general state of opinion in Britain was rather buried.

Seen in retrospect, the film hardly appears the 'subversive travesty' it was subsequently accused of being. But the timing could scarcely have been worse, and this time, in her flat in 10 Downing Street, Mrs Thatcher *was* watching. She saw George Foulkes labelling the sending of the task force 'a crazy reaction' and Tam Dalyell asking why, if the Argentines were as 'unpleasant' as she claimed, Britain had, in the last twenty years, 'traded with them, welcomed many of their most senior people from the Junta in this

country and sold them arms all the time'; she saw one of her own
MPs, David Crouch, warning that 'if the war goes on . . . we may be
judged to be standing on our dignity for a colonial ideal', while
another Tory back-bencher, Sir Anthony Meyer, his voice breaking,
made an appeal for peace:

> Once you get into a war situation, anybody who says 'For God's
> sake, let's stop it' is labelled as a defeatist. This is a label that you
> . . . you have to face up to it. My experience in the war was no
> worse than anybody else's, except that all my friends were
> killed. . . . I saw the effect that it had on their families, and it left
> me with a horror of war which goes very, very deep. I just . . . if
> our national survival is at stake, yes, clearly, we have to fight. If
> we're faced with the Russians—I'm not a disarmer or a
> unilateralist—if we're faced with the Russian threat, of course
> we fight. But anything short of that—I don't believe that killing
> can ever be the right answer.

'I think the principles involved are quite clear,' commented Eduardo
Crawley:

> Let me put it like this. Principle number one is that one cannot
> tolerate the occupation of part of one's territory by a foreign
> power, and it is perfectly legitimate to try to expel the intruder;
> principle number two is that one cannot negotiate sovereignty
> under duress, namely while somebody else is occupying part
> of one's territory; principle number three, it is wrong to flout a
> resolution by the United Nations Security Council; this puts one
> out of international law, so to speak.
>
> Now, odd as it may seem to the British public, these are
> precisely Argentina's arguments. . . .

Finally, the Prime Minister—'transfixed' is how one source
described her—heard Cockerell describe how one of her 'former
Cabinet Ministers with excellent Ministry of Defence contacts told
me that there had been reservations from the start about the
Falklands mission by the Chiefs of Staff', specifically Sir Michael
Beetham, Chief of the Air Staff.

Following the film there was a studio interview lasting about ten
minutes with Cecil Parkinson, the Conservative Party Chairman. It
was noticeable that Parkinson made no reference to the film despite
the fact that he had been sitting watching it. 'And that is all from
Panorama for this evening,' said Kee at the conclusion of the

programme. 'Until next week, when we will again probably be discussing the Falklands crisis in, we hope, a different mood, good night and'—he added with prophetic finality—'goodbye.'

Reactions to the programme were immediate and almost unanimously hostile. About four hundred callers rang to register complaints, but these represented perhaps only half of the total, as hundreds more found the lines to the BBC's duty office jammed. Those who did get through had to wait on average twenty minutes to register their views; some waited almost an hour. The BBC's Manchester newsroom alone took over forty calls. The complaints began within a couple of minutes of the programme's going on the air (these were objections to the interview with the Argentine Minister), and the last were still being logged in the early hours of the following morning. Other complainants turned to Fleet Street. *The Times* reported 'a number of people' who rang it to complain. The *Sun* remade its front page: 'OUTRAGE OVER THE BEEB!' proclaimed the banner headline: 'Storm at Panorama's "despicable" Argie bias'. The paper reported 'dozens of patriots' who rang and 'branded *Panorama* a "bloody disgrace".... former Cabinet Minister Geoffrey Rippon called it "one of the most despicable programmes it has ever been my misfortune to witness".'

Mary Whitehouse issued a statement calling the programme 'arrogant and disloyal': 'It prostituted the power their profession gives as broadcasters. To spread alarm and despondency was a treasonable offence in the last war. One wonders what succour this sort of broadcasting gives the people of Argentina.'

At the House of Commons, a group of Conservative MPs led by Eldon Griffiths, Anthony Grant and Peter Mills tabled a motion entitled 'Anti-British Broadcasting by the BBC':

> This House, having provided that the BBC shall enjoy all the benefits of broadcasting on the basis of a compulsory levy on the public and in the context of a democratic society whose freedoms require to be defended if they are to endure, records its dismay that some BBC programmes on the Falklands give the impression of being pro-Argentine and anti-Britain, while others appear to suggest that the invasion of these British islands is a matter in which the BBC is entitled to remain loftily neutral: and calls on the Corporation, if it cannot speak up for Britain, at least not to speak against it.

'I told you this would happen. See what you've done,' said Kee to Cockerell and Shawcross the following day.

That morning in *The Times* John Page returned to the attack on *Newsnight*, referring to Peter Snow's 'superior tone of super-neutrality which so many of us find objectionable and unacceptable'. Perhaps, he wondered, it might be possible to set up some kind of independent complaints board to monitor the BBC?

Prime Minister's questions were due to be taken at 3.15 that afternoon. Any hopes the BBC may have entertained that *Panorama* would not be brought up were swiftly dashed. Mrs Sally Oppenheim, a former Minister in Mrs Thatcher's Government, rose to denounce the previous night's *Panorama* as 'an odious, subversive travesty in which Michael Cockerell and other BBC reporters dishonoured the right to freedom of speech in this country', and to ask: 'Is it not time that such people accepted the fact that if they have these rights, they also have responsibilities?' Having seen the programme and anticipated the question, Mrs Thatcher had carefully rehearsed her remarks:

THE PRIME MINISTER: I share the deep concern that has been expressed on many sides, particularly about the content of yesterday evening's *Panorama* programme. I know how strongly many people feel that the case for our country is not being put with sufficient vigour on certain—I do not say all—BBC programmes. The chairman of the BBC has assured us, and has said in vigorous terms, that the BBC is not neutral on this point, and I hope his words will be heeded by the many who have responsibilities for standing up for our task force, our boys, our people and the cause of democracy.

MR WINNICK (Labour MP for Walsall North): Does not the Prime Minister agree that one of the virtues of a political democracy is that radio and television should be independent from constant Government control and interference? Would it not be useful if some of her right hon. and hon. Friends stopped their constant intimidation of the BBC? Perhaps the Prime Minister would take the hint as well?

THE PRIME MINISTER: It is our great pride that the British media are free. We ask them, when the lives of some of our people may be at stake through information or through discussions that can be of use to the enemy—(*Interruption*)—to take that into account on their programmes. It is our pride that we have no censorship. That is the essence of a free country. But we expect the case for freedom to be put by those who are responsible for doing so.

The ultra-patriotic Sir Bernard Braine ('Braine of Britain', as he is known), who had earlier said that the Argentine occupation was enough 'to make any normal Englishman's blood boil', was quickly on his feet. Has the Prime Minister, he thundered over a swelling chorus of cheers and boos, 'been made aware of the rising tide of anger among our constituents at the media treatment and presentation of enemy propaganda and the defeatist views of an unrepresentative minority? Is she aware that an increasing number of people are telling us that this amounts to a sort of treachery?' At the word 'treachery' there was a minor eruption, with Conservative MPs waving their arms and pointing at Tam Dalyell and Tony Benn sitting on the Labour benches. 'Our people,' said the Prime Minister, when the din had subsided, 'are very robust and the heart of Britain is sound. I hope that individually they will make their views directly known to the BBC, by their letters and telephone calls.' The Labour leader, Michael Foot, entered the fray. The Prime Minister's remarks, he said, were 'concerned with the important matter of how freedom of discussion is to be conducted in this country'. 'Some of us', he added to loud Labour cheers, 'are determined to defend it.' He went on:

> Before the right hon. Lady pursues further her strictures of the BBC, where I am sure people are seeking to do their duty in difficult circumstances, will she take some steps to reprove the attitude of some newspapers that support her—the hysterical bloodlust of the *Sun* and the *Daily Mail*, which bring such disgrace on the journalism of this country?
> THE PRIME MINISTER: ... The media are totally free to discuss and publish what they wish. Equally, as the right hon. Gentleman has demonstrated, we are free to say what we think about them.

Before the exchanges could progress any further, Tam Dalyell rose to make a point of order which brought the afternoon to its noisy climax. Sir Bernard Braine, he said, had referred to himself and the other Labour MP who took part in *Panorama*, George Foulkes, as traitors, while Mrs Oppenheim had referred to 'dishonour': 'Some of us who have been in the 7th Armoured Division, who have been gunner operators on tanks and many of whose contemporaries in training were shot up with the King's Royal Irish Hussars in Korea, take it ill to be accused of treachery and dishonour.' Uproar ensued as MP after MP rose to try to make points of order. The Speaker suggested that 'it would be in the interests of the House if, during these difficult days when there is severe tension both here and in the country, we tried to avoid the words "treachery" and "treason", and such things, because they advance nobody's argument.' Refusing to take any further points of order, he brought Prime Minister's Question Time to an abrupt end. Later that same day a group of furious Conservative MPs surrounded Sir Anthony Meyer in a corridor. 'You are a disgrace', said one of them, 'to your school, your regiment and your country.'

The row was given extensive coverage in the press. In the absence of any pictures or much news from the South Atlantic, here was a fight in which everyone could take part. It was a gift to Fleet Street cartoonists. The *Daily Mail* showed Mrs Thatcher as a television newsreader: 'Here is the news. There has been a shake-up at the BBC.' The *Daily Express* depicted a studio set labelled 'Traitorama' and a discussion between the Kaiser, Admiral Tirpitz and Generals Hindenberg and Ludendorff: 'If Britain admits German sovereignty over the "British" Isles,' says one, 'we'll stop the war.' In the *Mirror* a family watches as its television blows up with the caption 'Her Majesty's Government regrets the necessary destruction of your set, but points out you were tuned to the BBC.' In the *Sun* the BBC newsreader is an Argentinian, complete with sombrero and Zapata moustache: ''Ello! 'Ere's ze latest unbiased news on ze Falklands crisis.'

John Stokes, Conservative MP for Halesowen and Stourbridge, writing to *The Times* about the BBC, lamented 'the apparent inability of its management to *supervise* producers properly'. Sir Angus Maude, a former Cabinet Minister in charge of overseeing the Government's media 'image', complained that the BBC 'seemed to be deliberately combing the world to find people who could be persuaded to say that almost everything the British Government did was either militarily dangerous or diplomatically inept'. 'Whatever happened to the BBC Voice of Britain?' asked an article in the *Daily Mail*, suggesting that the Corporation was politically biased and run by 'lightweight liberal intellectuals'.

Most newspapers picked up a remark made by the Managing Director of BBC Radio, Richard Francis, who told the International Press Institute in Madrid:

> feelings of humanity apart, to report the resilient reaction of the Argentine people to the losses among their armed forces provides an important element of the picture for the British people. The widow of Portsmouth is no different from the widow of Buenos Aires. The BBC needs no lesson in patriotism.

The *Sun* suggested that 'smug Mr Francis should be down on his plump knees, giving thanks' that he wasn't living in Argentina, where journalists were 'kidnapped, terrorized and beaten and then dumped practically naked'.

Yet despite all the abuse, the BBC refused to yield. This surprised some. In the past it has not always been so deaf to political criticism. But Sir Ian Trethowan, the Director-General, was away at that time, and in his absence his designated successor, Alasdair Milne, remained firm. 'We might increase our popularity by appearing jingoistic,' he said in an interview with the London *Standard* on 12 May, 'but then no one would believe what we were saying. I do not intend to trade our reputation to please such critics.' The BBC, he claimed, is 'the British Voice of Truth':

> The notion that we are traitors is outrageous. There is no one in the BBC who does not agree that the Argentines committed aggression. But this is not total war. One day we will be negotiating with the enemy so we must try to understand them. We at the BBC have re-examined our broad policy and will not change it. We have no sense of guilt or failure.

A few hours after the article appeared, Milne's resolve was to be given a severe testing in the last set-piece battle between the BBC and the Conservative Party during the Falklands war.

The Tory Media Committee normally attracts only a handful of MPs to its meetings, but on the night of Wednesday, 12 May, more than a hundred crowded into Committee Room 13 at the House of Commons to what was advertised as an opportunity to 'exchange views' with George Howard and Alasdair Milne but turned into what one blood-spattered participant later described as 'an ox-roast'. 'You have to understand', says one 'wet' Tory backbencher, 'that as far as most Conservatives are concerned, the BBC is at best a collection of Hampstead liberals. At worst, it's a Marxist conspiracy.'

The two BBC men were, at first sight, totally dissimilar. Milne, a professional broadcaster all his life and still only in his early fifties, is a product of Winchester and New College, Oxford, a man renowned for a forensic intellect and a cutting tongue. Howard, 62, ex-Eton, ex-Balliol, is a wealthy landowner, a former officer in the Green Howards (the family regiment) and owner of Castle Howard. There was an unspoken arrogance in both men which provoked additional anger within some sections of the Tory Party.

From the outset it was accusations rather than questions that were hurled at the two men from a violently hostile meeting. Milne tried to answer:

> The first time I spoke [he recalled later], they barked, 'Can't hear you!', so I said I'd speak up. Then they shouted, 'Still can't hear you. Stand up!' It was like being in the Star Chamber. When they got really angry, they started waving their order papers and growling like dogs.

Milne was not cowed—he was furious. After the first few minutes he took no further part in the proceedings. 'He sat there,' says one MP who was at the meeting, 'a small figure, hunched and saturnine, with an expression of mixed incredulity, contempt and anger.'

The main job of tackling the criticisms fell to the bulky figure of George Howard, 'who stood like an eighteenth-century Whig grandee—which in many ways is what he is—confronted by a group of angry tradesmen and looking as though he'd like to set the dogs on them'. Normally Howard has a reputation for wearing shirts with the pattern and texture of sofa covers, but in honour of this occasion he was soberly dressed in dark suit and tie.

The first part of the meeting was devoted fairly specifically to attacks on the *Panorama* programme. The denunciations then moved into the broader areas of the BBC's coverage, with furious attacks from such figures as Winston Churchill, Alan Clark and John Biggs-Davison. Churchill in particular attacked the remarks of Richard Francis, claiming that 'at least the widow of Portsmouth pays a licence fee.' Howard tried to quote the precedent of the Second World War. To roars of 'Hear hear!' and the banging of desk tops, Churchill mocked that at least then the BBC hadn't given equal time to Dr Goebbels: 'I suggested he should have the courage to sack those responsible for *Panorama* or offer his own resignation. He ducked that one.' 'He was kicked all round the room,' said one MP of Howard. 'It was the most appalling, lamentable and disgraceful performance. There was no apology or contrition.'

At the end of an hour, MPs streamed out of one door, while Milne, white with rage, and Howard, his face dripping with sweat, slipped out of another, heading, it was widely believed, for the more congenial atmosphere of William Whitelaw's office.

The descriptions of the private meeting given out that night by MPs read like the type of one-line reviews normally found outside cinemas showing horror films: 'Blood and entrails all over the place', 'They were roasted alive', 'They went for their throats'. 'We have seen the whites of each other's eyes,' commented Geoffrey Johnson Smith, the chairman of the meeting. To Sir Hector Monroe, former Sports Minister, it was 'the ugliest meeting I have ever attended in my years as an MP'.

It was a tribal ritual of a sort which only the English ruling-class male, with his experience of public-school raggings, could have mounted; in retrospect it can be seen to have exposed and destroyed the Conservative right's witch-hunt against the BBC virtually overnight. Neither Milne nor Howard had shifted their ground, yet from this point onwards there was to be little more criticism of the BBC. It was as if someone had thrown a switch. The MPs drifted away and seemed purged of their anger. Milne and Howard were left to lick their wounds. Milne, according to Geoffrey Johnson Smith, simply seemed profoundly unimpressed with the intellectual calibre of the arguments put up against him'. Howard told reporters afterwards: 'I am not prepared to apologize for the programme.' According to the *Observer*, the main injury was to his dignity. He objected to newspaper reports of him mopping his brow as if in terror: 'It was very, very hot in that room.' The extent to which the poison had been drawn can be gathered from the fact that the following week, Sir Ian Trethowan, now back at the BBC, paid a visit himself to the Commons and was heard in respectful silence by an all-party meeting of MPs.

A week which had begun badly for the BBC ended remarkably well. *The Times*, the *Guardian* and the *Daily Mirror* all carried editorials supporting the corporation. So too did a number of regional papers, including the *Yorkshire Post* and the *Glasgow Herald*. A clear signal to the militant right of his Party to calm down came on Friday from the Leader of the House of Commons, John Biffen. He told Conservatives in Scotland that, 'like the freedom of dissent and debate in Parliament, free speech is a bulwark of the national liberty which the Conservative Party has always defended.' The most unexpected statement, but perhaps the most significant, came from the Prince of Wales. On 14 May, in a speech given at the Open University before an audience which included George Howard, he praised the British media for being made up of 'independent personalities' and 'not servants of the state machine'. He admitted they might 'get it wrong from time to time', but added, 'My goodness, you certainly can't please everybody.'

The only fly in this soothing ointment, as far as the BBC was concerned, was Robert Kee. On the day that John Biffen and Prince Charles made their contributions to the debate, Kee made his in a letter to *The Times* attacking *Panorama*:

> I am naturally grateful to the Chairman and Director-General-designate of the BBC [he wrote] for loyally defending me among other colleagues against criticism of the film section in that programme, but wish to release them from the obligation in my own case since I must dissociate myself from the defence.

Kee revealed that he had been so unhappy with the 'poor objective journalism' of the film that he had actually considered disowning it live on air, 'but in the interests of immediate programme solidarity decided not to'.

Kee had taken over as presenter of *Panorama* at a salary of around £1,000 per programme the previous January. It had not proved an especially happy arrangement from the beginning, and the 62-year-old presenter had made a shaky start to the Falklands war, first in a carping and much criticized interview with Lord Carrington immediately after the latter's resignation on 5 April, and then, in the edition before the controversial 'anti-war' programme, in an interview with the Prime Minister considered by many to be excessively obsequious. After his letter to *The Times*, which breached the agreement under which he was employed, the BBC decided to suspend Kee for a month, pending a decision about his future. To his colleagues on *Panorama* it seemed a maliciously ill-timed moment to attack them, just as the argument about Monday's programme appeared to be over. They made it clear that they would be unhappy at having to work with him again, and Kee, under contract anyway to the new breakfast programme *TV-AM*, resigned. He never presented *Panorama* again. It was a bitter end to an association with the BBC spanning almost a quarter of a century, which had included a highly praised series on the history of Ireland.

The noisiest attacks on the BBC may have come from the right, but the broadcasters were also under continual fire from the left. On 9 May the Ad Hoc Falkland Islands Peace Committee (a pressure group composed of nineteen organizations, including the Campaign for Nuclear Disarmament and the United Nations Association) wrote to the BBC setting out its belief that 'the coverage of the Falklands Islands conflict has been biased towards the military viewpoint to the detriment of the minority view, which calls for an immediate truce, negotiations and a stop to this war.' Tony Benn repeatedly insisted that the media were deliberately ignoring 'the people in this country who want the war to end'. The Glasgow Media Group, persistent left-wing critics of television news coverage, claim to show that the peace groups were given a disproportionately small amount of publicity by comparison with their size and importance.

The BBC found its supporters in the centre of the political spectrum. The Liberal leader, David Steel, and the SDP MP William Rodgers tabled a Commons motion on 11 May regretting the 'intemperate attacks' made on the BBC: 'These attacks are deeply distasteful to many of those members who have hitherto given the Government steady support.' Even within the Conservative Party it was noticeable that certain senior figures appeared to be distancing themselves from the Prime Minister: William Whitelaw, as Home Secretary the Minister ultimately responsible for the BBC, was eloquent in his complete silence on the subject; John Biffen went out of his way to defend the principle of free speech; and Francis Pym, while suggesting that members of the public should write to the BBC if they had any complaints, pointedly remarked: 'It is not for me to express a view, even if I had one.' Add Prince Charles and the editorial support of *The Times* and the *Sunday Times*, and it is clear that the Establishment moved swiftly to protect one of its own kind.

This appeal to the centre goes beyond mere sympathy for the BBC as an organization. Television, as William S. Paley, the man who created CBS, has remarked, is itself a *consensus* medium. In its news coverage it reflects and consolidates accepted beliefs. It does little to help foster new ways of thinking. Hence its persistent critics are generally to be found on the radical fringes of politics. If the BBC has had a rougher time than usual over the last few years, that is mainly because of the arrival on the scene of a Prime Minister very much *not* in the consensus mould, along with the general ascendency of militants in both major parties. The reaction of these groups to the television coverage of the Falklands war was symptomatic of a much more deeply rooted hostility.

If politicians tended to respond according to type, what did the average viewer make of television's coverage and the row which surrounded it? Undoubtedly the argument made an appeal to a certain type of right-wing nationalism lurking behind many a suburban lace curtain. 'You snide bastard,' ran one typical letter to Michael Cockerell. 'We're sick and tired of you lefties sitting in your cushy jobs and not having the decency to remember your duty as an Englishman. . . . We want and expect loyalty and patriotism from our reporters in emergencies like this. You'd better watch it, you overbearing prejudiced creep.' But every reporter and producer occasionally receives such letters (for some reason often in green ink on lined paper). The BBC switchboard had been jammed often enough before the Falklands war, possibly from the same people, following programmes on subjects like immigration.

It is impossible to estimate how many letters and phone calls came as a direct result of the Foreign Secretary's and the Prime Minister's call to the public to make its views known to the BBC. Anger is a much stronger feeling than satisfaction, and because of the effort required to register a view, the number of complaints is inevitably in excess of the number of compliments. Even so, in an interview with Chris Dunkley published in the *Financial Times* on 15 May, Alasdair Milne claimed: 'On the night after the Media Committee row we had 251 against us but 200 ringing in support. That's most unusual.' The claims made by some Conservative MPs about the number of letters they were receiving from constituents who were hostile to the BBC may also have been exaggerated. 'Because I'm a former chairman of the Media Committee,' says Julian Critchley, the Conservative MP for Aldershot, 'I reckon to get more letters about this sort of thing than most MPs. During the whole of the war I received just one letter complaining about the BBC.'

Further support for the theory that the attacks on the BBC were unrepresentative of the mood of the country as a whole can be seen in two opinion polls commissioned at the time. An independent survey carried out for the BBC by the Audience Selection company found that 81 per cent of 1,049 viewers and listeners questioned thought that the BBC had behaved 'in a responsible manner in its coverage of the Falklands crisis'; only 14 per cent thought it had not been 'responsible'. The same proportion, 81 per cent, thought the BBC should 'pursue its traditional policy of reflecting the full range of opinions'; 10 per cent thought it should not. The poll was conducted on Thursday, 13 May, after the controversial *Panorama* and *Newsnight* programmes and the attacks in the Commons.

The following week, a poll conducted by Gallup for the *Daily Telegraph* was slightly less favourable but still broadly reinforced the earlier findings. Sixty-two per cent thought the Corporation was reporting the crisis fairly; 22 per cent thought it was not. When broken down according to political affiliation, the poll showed clearly that the closer to the centre of the political spectrum, the greater the support for the BBC:

> *Question*: The BBC in particular have been criticized for not fairly representing the British point of view. Do you think this criticism is or is not justified?

	Con.	Lab.	Lib.	SDP
	%	%	%	%
Is	32	25	26	12
Is not	57	61	64	71

One of the justifications for the attack on television was that it gave aid and comfort to the enemy not merely by reporting his point of view, but also by the amount of harmful speculation about military options it fuelled. Both networks had a stage army òf retired military officers who appeared regularly to give their views of the significance of events in the South Atlantic. 'We had a smallish band of people,' said the editor of ITN, 'who, like World Cup commentators, we had as part of the essential team.' On 29 April Mrs Thatcher expressed her unhappiness with this stream of semi-informed comment. 'Everything they say', she told Parliament, 'may put someone's life in jeopardy.'

The notion that Argentina might pick up useful ideas from these discussions was flatly rejected by the broadcasters. 'Argentine intelligence just isn't that defective,' claimed Milne. That is also the private view of senior officials inside the Ministry of Defence now that the war is over. An enormous amount of technical data about British weapon systems is available from unclassified sources such as Jane's books on ships and aircraft. At one point ITN set out to do a story showing how much information was available simply in the trade press of the international arms industry. 'In the event the story was squeezed,' lamented David Nicholas after the war. 'I regret that we did not do that. I think the public would have understood how much more readily accessible this information was.'

The Argentines certainly should have been aware of our fighting capability. Not only did we sell them a large amount of our military hardware, but we also laid on demonstrations of specific items, such as the Harrier jet, in an effort to persuade them to buy. Nor were retired officers likely to think up many strategic ideas which would not have already occurred to the Argentines themselves. As Sir Frank Cooper pointed out:

> Anyone who looked at the map would see it is not as though there are vast numbers of population centres or vast numbers of roads. I think there are 60 miles of paved roads in all the Falkland Islands—no, less than that. You do not need to be a genius to start speculating: the range of military options was indeed a fairly narrow one.

It would have greatly suited the Government if the media had confined themselves to straight reporting of the very limited amount of hard news which was available about the Falklands campaign, completely ignored what was going on in Argentina, and left it at that. But such an idea seemed preposterous to the broadcasters. At a time of enormous world interest they would have had to cut back their news and current affairs output: they could not have filled the programmes with what was officially available. But beyond that, the networks understandably felt a *duty* to inform the public.

The attack on television, which started and ended so abruptly, coincided with a period of doubt about the wisdom of sending the task force—doubt which some programmes reflected. This nervous atmosphere, coupled with a long-standing antipathy towards the BBC among certain Conservative back-benchers, produced a week-long crisis in relations between the Corporation and the Government. The BBC was singled out for attack rather than ITN because it has more resources for reporting foreign news and because it produces, in programmes like *Newsnight* and *Panorama*, many more hours of news and current affairs. It is also a British institution, publicly owned, with a unique history and reputation.

The BBC was caught in a pincer attack: the Ministry of Defence and the lack of news and pictures of the task force on one flank; the Conservative Party with a demand for more 'helpful' coverage on the other. The Falklands crisis reinforced the lesson of 1940 and 1956: that in time of war a conflict of interests inevitably exists between the Government and the BBC.

6. The Ministry of Truth

The battle between the BBC and the Government was given extensive coverage in the rest of the world's media. The *Guardian*'s Harold Jackson reported from Washington:

> The recent parliamentary row about the BBC's handling of the crisis was reported by American television in much the way it might have reported the tribal rites of Borneo headhunters—as a weird quirk, surviving unsuspected in the modern world. . . . This American view of war reporting stems not only from the First Amendment guarantee of a fair press, but from a simple democratic conviction that the taxpayer has a right to know how his money is being spent and to express his opinion about it.

Sir Bernard Braine startled American audiences when he appeared on US network television to denounce *Panorama* as 'the pathway to anarchy'.

The BBC row illustrated the contrast between the position of the media in this country and the constitutionally safeguarded role of the press in the United States. Paul Scott Mowrer, editor of the *Chicago Daily News*, defined the duty of the press as it is seen in American eyes in a speech made during the Second World War: 'The final political decision rests with the people. And the people, so that they may make up their minds, must be given the facts, even in war time, or, perhaps, *especially* in war time.' It is clear that in many respects the British people were *not* given the facts during the Falklands war. Information was handed out slowly and often reluctantly by the Ministry of Defence; rumours were allowed to circulate unchecked; and the British authorities frequently used the media as an instrument with which to confuse the enemy.

The military commanders were quite open about their intention of making use of the press. According to John Witherow, Captain Jeremy Black told the *Invincible* journalists that they were 'one of the weapons systems in the fight against Argentina'. When *Hermes* left Ascension, Brian Hanrahan recalled:

> We had a chat with the Admiral, Admiral Woodward, who said it was his intention to try and cause as much confusion to the enemy as possible; he intended to keep them guessing about what he intended, where he intended to do it and what means he intended to deploy and if there was any way in which he could use us as part of that attempt to confuse the enemy, he intended to do so.

Woodward happily confirmed the conversation:

> As I remember it, I probably said words to the effect that all is fair in love and war, and a military man for military reasons should be prepared to use misinformation, as we call it; but I think I probably qualified it by saying, perhaps as a result of conversation with Mr Hanrahan and Mr Nicholson, that I quite recognized this might be politically unacceptable.

Newsmen, said the Chief of the Defence Staff, Sir Terence Lewin, after the war, were 'most helpful with our deception plans'.

'Deception' and 'misinformation' are recognized military techniques in which the British have long experience. 'In wartime,' Churchill told Stalin in his famous comment at Teheran in 1943, 'truth is so precious that she should always be attended by a bodyguard of lies.' During the Second World War there were many examples of official concealment or outright lying to the press. The British Air Ministry exaggerated the known number of enemy planes shot down during the Battle of Britain by one-third. During the 'Crusader' tank battle in North Africa, the British claimed to have destroyed more tanks than Rommel actually possessed. German claims that we were deliberately bombing their civilians rather than their military installations were true but were dismissed as 'propaganda'. The extent of our military defeats in France in 1940, in Greece and at Dieppe were all concealed. When correspondents described the situation at Anzio in 1944 as 'desperate', Churchill told the Commons that 'such words as "desperate" ought not to be used about the position in a battle of this kind where they are false. Still less should they be used if they were true.'

A generation later, in 1982, this was still the official view. But the difference was that this was not Total War in which the morale of a munitions worker had to be nurtured as much as a commando's. This was a limited action. The two sides never even declared war. Yet the military reacted as if national survival were at stake. When Sir Terence Lewin was asked whether 'deceiving the press or deceiving the public through the press is reasonable ... on grounds of operational security or morale', he replied:

> I do not see it as deceiving the press or the public; I see it as deceiving the enemy. What I am trying to do is to win. Anything I can do to help me win is fair as far as I am concerned, and I would have thought that that was what the Government and the public and the media would want too, provided the outcome was the one we were all after.

The omission of certain crucial pieces of information, the decision to restrict press briefings to a minimum, the censorship on grounds of taste as well as on grounds of security—all created an image of the war in the British media which often bore little relation to the truth. 'I looked in the newspapers,' said Max Hastings on his return from the Falklands, 'and was simply staggered to see what a load of complete misinformation was being transmitted.' This policy, combined with the fact that only British reporters were allowed to sail with the task force, had ramifications that extended beyond Britain itself. The Vice-President of one American network news organization told ITN:

> The British press was discounted here as a reliable source of news all during the Falklands engagement. It was understood, although not really mentioned, that there were a lot more things going on than the press reported and that therefore there was a form of lying going on. Not necessarily the lying of telling false facts but saying misleading things for devious purposes. What was reported would have been believed here if there were Americans present.
>
> I mention this in part because to us as news executives one of the most annoying parts of it all was to rely so heavily on so few people who had no connection with our news operations. But that is a parochial concern which is not necessarily a problem for any Parliament. What should be a problem for those in Parliament is that the Government always wants to be believed but in circumstances like that, it won't be. A prescription for

disbelief is easy to write: don't let any nation in; be obvious in your manipulation of what the reporters there say; protest that you are the home of the free and the land of the brave.

Basically, I think it is any nation's right to run its war any way it likes. What it ought not to expect is that others will believe its protestations when it does so in a foolish way.

Britain, said Alan Protheroe towards the end of the Falklands conflict, 'lost the information war'.

It was the Ministry of Defence in London which was held to be chiefly responsible for the poor quality of the coverage and for several incidents which either bordered on, or manifestly were, the result of 'misinformation'.

The official in charge of the MoD's public relations department when the Falklands crisis began was, by a fluke of timing, a man with no formal training in handling the press. Ian McDonald, 46 years old, is a career civil servant who has spent his entire working life in the MoD, having joined it after graduating with a degree in English and Greek from Glasgow University. After years of steady promotion he had become, by 1979, the assistant secretary in charge of Division 14, the Ministry's recruitment and pay section. Although not a post renowned for requiring a detailed knowledge of the world's media, three years ago McDonald abruptly moved across to become the Ministry of Defence's deputy chief of public relations (DCPR).

Public relations officers in Whitehall belong to a structure that is separate from the department in which they happen to work, administered by the Central Office of Information. The post of DCPR at the MoD was an historical aberration outside this system, created after the Labour Defence Secretary, Fred Mulley, was photographed asleep at an RAF ceremony attended by the Queen. The job of DCPR was created specifically in order that an able professional civil servant could act as a personal PR shield for Mulley. But when Mulley left, the post was not abolished. Instead a classic case of bureaucratic evolution ensued. The position of DCPR was enhanced by the presence of a weak chief of public relations and by the fact that its occupant had constant access to the main source of power, the Secretary of State. Additional duties were added. By the time McDonald took over, DCPR was responsible for handling the media in all matters relating to nuclear weapons. 'It was a crazy situation,' says one senior Whitehall information officer. 'I don't

know how any professional PR man worth his salt could put up with
it.'

When the post of chief of public relations fell vacant at the end of
1981, McDonald applied for it. He was considered to have a good
chance, if only because he was one of the few MoD civil servants to
enjoy a close personal association with the prickly John Nott. But
McDonald was passed over. The job went instead to Neville Taylor,
the favoured candidate of the Prime Minister's press secretary,
Bernard Ingham. Because of illness and a backlog of work at his old
job as head of PR at the Department of Health and Social Security,
Taylor was unable to take up his new post immediately. It was agreed
that McDonald should continue as acting head of PR at the MoD
until June 1982. It was in this state of bureaucratic confusion that the
Ministry of Defence public relations department suddenly found
itself caught up in the most hectic crisis in its history.

To deal with the world's media, McDonald had working to him
three service directors of public relations—military officers
principally responsible for liaising with service PR men scattered
among the British forces around the world—a further four
servicemen and eighteen civilian press officers. In the initial rush to
arrange accreditation, McDonald also had to try to lash together
some sort of information policy to present to Nott. 'I can remember
very distinctly', he said later, 'that there was a time at which I closed
the door of my office and locked it and sat trying to think it out for
five minutes.'

The plan McDonald emerged with was a novel one. Most
journalists were expecting the Ministry of Defence to provide extra
facilities. McDonald decided to *cut back* drastically on the MoD's
contacts with the media. Hitherto, defence correspondents had been
kept informed of the general direction of the Ministry's policy by
means of regular off-the-record briefings with the Permanent Under-
Secretary, Sir Frank Cooper: these were to be stopped. Information
was to be rationed strictly to official statements, which would be
issued each day at noon by McDonald. Apart from this, no
information was to be communicated to the media. There were three
central reasons for this clamp-down, as McDonald later explained:

> First of all, we ourselves, and the Chiefs of Staff, were working
> out what to do; there was no absolute plan at that stage; it was
> being formulated.... Secondly, at that time the main initiative

was with the Foreign Office and with diplomacy. The task force was seen very much as an adjunct to that diplomacy. The Foreign Office was having its regular briefings, and therefore it seemed to me that the MoD ... could restrict itself to on-the-record briefings. The third thing was the security aspect. There was a very strong feeling that in fact to talk about where the Fleet, the task force, was, how it was being split up as it sailed to the Falkland Islands, would be to give information to the Argentines about possible intentions. I did not see how, talking unattributably off the record, we would be able to avoid trespassing on those kinds of areas.

McDonald simply stopped speaking privately to the press, and he instructed everyone else in his department to do the same.

The press took the cancellation of background briefings badly. It laid the foundations, wrote the Press Association, for 'the loss of credibility from which [the] MoD never recovered'. Some defence correspondents, dependent on being spoon-fed information in non-attributable briefings, were left with nothing to say. Even many conscientious journalists were wrong-footed. Over recent years the only battles spoken of in the Ministry of Defence have been those fought over budgets and Treasury forecasts. The last thing many *defence* correspondents expected to have to write about was a *war*. 'Today we have a new breed of defence correspondent,' says one official, 'who is much more adept at writing about things like cash limits than warfare. The Falklands hit this type of journalist amidships.'

Tony Smith, the defence correspondent of the *Daily Star*, wrote that the press was 'enraged that normal practice was not carried out.... we were given no more information than the man from *Pravda*.' The blackout extended to the most respected correspondents. 'In normal times,' claimed Jim Meacham of the *Economist*, 'I could call up the Chief of Public Relations and ask how many tanks are in Germany and he would tell me, within reasonable tolerance. During the Falkland Islands war they would not tell me if there were any tanks in Germany or even if there was a Germany.' Members of the Foreign Press Association attacked 'the high-handed or indifferent attitude' of the MoD and claimed that the 'inadequacy' of the briefings led 'to Argentine sources exercising undue influence in the foreign press'.

The refusal of the MoD to give the media guidance did nothing to stop speculation. Indeed, as David Fairhall, the defence correspondent of the *Guardian*, pointed out, 'it was sometimes the lack of real information that led, rightly or wrongly, to speculation about tactics.' McDonald's policy—which was approved by Sir Frank Cooper and John Nott—fostered a climate in which rumour festered and the press became highly suggestible.

When the crisis began, newspapers reported that HMS *Superb*, one of Britain's nuclear-powered hunter-killer submarines, was on her way to the Falklands. Where did this story originate? No one seems able to remember. It was suggested that the submarine was seen leaving Gibraltar, and then that a Conservative MP, following a briefing by the junior Foreign Minister, Richard Luce, told the press that *a* submarine was on her way south. It somehow became accepted as fact and illustrates how, in the absence of hard news, the press feeds off itself. Jon Connell, defence correspondent of the *Sunday Times*, describes the process:

> Because information was so thin one was picking it up sometimes from one's colleagues, sometimes from reading other newspapers and getting what were not really confirmations but probably talking to somebody in the House or somebody in the MoD who might indicate, yes, there was a submarine on the way, or something to that effect. I cannot precisely remember in that instance what it was that made us print it.

It later emerged that *Superb* was undergoing repairs at her base in Scotland. Yet whenever the journalists asked McDonald to confirm that *Superb* was in the South Atlantic, he refused to comment. The MoD's defence was that it never reveals the positions of its submarines. But to the press it looked as if they had been misled deliberately: it was, after all, useful for the British to have the Argentine Navy believe there was a submarine lurking close by to deter it from venturing out of harbour. 'We were positively and unquestionably encouraged', claimed Jim Meacham, 'to think (and write) that this nuclear submarine had gone south.' The result, as Connell observed, was to make the defence correspondents look 'pretty silly . . . because obviously our sources were not good'.

For hard news of what was happening the media had to rely on McDonald's attributable noon briefings. At their inception he made two promises to the journalists: he would not tell them 'an untruth', but neither would he say anything which might prejudice the success of the task force or jeopardize the lives of the men aboard it. In the interests of keeping the second promise, he came perilously close to breaking the first.

On the way to Ascension, *Invincible* developed severe problems with her engines. Rumours reached London, by way of American intelligence, that one of the carriers was in trouble. McDonald knew he would be asked a question and knew also that a 'no comment' would provoke a flurry of damaging speculation. But by an extraordinary stroke of luck the press had become convinced that it was the aged *Hermes* rather than the modern *Invincible* which was in difficulties. They asked: 'Is *Hermes* suffering from mechanical problems?' McDonald was able to deny it firmly and to bring the briefing swiftly to a close. It was not always so easy.

On Wednesday, 21 April, men of the Special Air Service (SAS) were landed on a glacier on the remote island of South Georgia. By the following morning they were in severe difficulties and three helicopters set off to rescue them. In blizzard conditions, with winds of up to 100 miles an hour, two of the helicopters crashed. No one was injured, but thirteen SAS men and four helicopter crewmen would have died in the freezing conditions had it not been for the skill of a single Wessex helicopter pilot in rescuing them.

In London, when the news first came through, it was thought that there were no survivors. 'You can imagine how we felt,' says one senior MoD official. 'This was the first real action of the war, and it was a terrible reversal. It provoked hideous memories of the American helicopter disaster when they tried to rescue the hostages in Iran.' The accident was so sensitive that it was agreed not even to raise it at the morning meeting of the Chiefs of Staff committee. With negotiations with Argentina still in progress, it was thought that the news of the disaster might change the mood in the country and the House of Commons. It might even lead to the recall of the task force.

It was in the full knowledge of what had happened on South Georgia that Ian McDonald faced the press on 24 April and told them: 'The task force has not landed anywhere.' Newspapers had already begun claiming that operations to recover South Georgia were under way. Sceptical reporters began to press McDonald. He refused to go any further or to define what he meant by 'the task force' or a 'landing'. Technically, McDonald insisted afterwards, he had not broken his pledge never to tell 'an untruth'. The SAS patrol, he argued, was not 'the task force'. The loss of the two helicopters emerged only by accident three weeks later, when a serviceman wrote home telling what had happened.

When South Georgia *was* recaptured on 25 April, the British public was given the morale-boosting but completely false impression that it had been an effortless victory. The defence correspondents were treated, said Meacham, to 'a fairly comprehensive briefing, we thought, by a Marine Corps officer at the Ministry of Defence with a great big map about how this went . . . . it certainly led us all to believe that the South Georgia operation had been a great success.'

In Downing Street that night Mrs Thatcher instructed the press to 'Rejoice!' In Parliament the next day she praised the 'professional skill' of what was portrayed as an operation of surgical precision. On board *Hermes* Admiral Woodward gave an interview in which he jubilantly described the near-fiasco on South Georgia as 'a walkover'.

The press reflected the official line. The *Daily Telegraph* called the British forces 'cockleshell heroes'. 'VICTORY: Quick-Fire Marines Grab Penguin Isle' was the headline in the *Daily Star*. 'VICTORY!' proclaimed the *Sun*, reprinting in large type Woodward's grandiloquent signal which began 'Be pleased to inform Her Majesty. . . .' The Government's triumph over the media was almost as great as the victory over Argentina. When Max Hastings on board *Canberra* read the newspapers a few days later he could hardly believe it:

> Reports published in the newspapers in London of the way in which South Georgia had been retaken were complete and absolute rubbish from beginning to end . . . they did nothing to help our credibility on the spot when members of the task force were reading them. One wondered who had been feeding them all this stuff. . . .

Meacham considered it 'one of the major disinformation operations of this campaign'.

With the onset of fighting, the pressures on the Ministry of Defence to provide information became far greater. The Falklands crisis was now the dominant news story in the world. Hundreds of British and foreign journalists had been assigned to cover it. Clearly, it was no longer possible to limit facilities to a single noon statement followed by a question-and-answer session, briefings from which television and radio were completely excluded. Accordingly, a week after the retaking of South Georgia, on Sunday, 2 May, the MoD opened an Emergency Press Centre—known as 'the concourse'—which had as its focus a large ground-floor room, appropriately decorated with a portrait of Horatio Nelson.

The Centre opened at 10 a.m. and closed at 10 p.m., although occasionally it remained in use throughout the night. Inside were a battery of telephones, including eight direct lines to the largest media organizations. Radio and television studios were housed inside the MoD and outside in temporary huts in the car park. Visual display units were installed, eventually capable of calling upon 1,250 pages of computerized information: journalists could summon up all previous official statements and answers to questions, particulars of task-force ships, biographies of senior officers—every detail, down to how many Chinese cooks were sailing with the fleet. Reporters had everything they needed except the one thing they wanted most: news.

Over it all presided the urbane and evasive McDonald. By the time he emerged on to the floor of the concourse at noon he had already been at work for more than four hours, and the short statement he would read was the collective product of more than a dozen hands.

It had its genesis at 7.30 a.m., when McDonald arrived at the Ministry of Defence to read through the morning newspapers and to prepare a short summary of their contents. At about 8.30 he would meet Sir Frank Cooper to discuss information policy and listen in while Cooper was briefed on the overnight situation by the MoD's night-duty staff. The first broad outline of what might be released to the media would begin to take shape.

From the MoD McDonald would walk across to 10 Downing Street for the daily meeting of the Information Co-ordination Group, chaired by Bernard Ingham. Here the British Government's overall public relations strategy was decided between a variety of interested officials, including Nicholas Fenn, head of PR at the Foreign Office, a representative from the Central Office of Information ('responsible', in the words of the MoD, 'for maintaining the information effort abroad'), an official from the Cabinet Office, and the private secretary to Cecil Parkinson, who, as the one member of the War Cabinet without a department to run, had become the Government's chief ministerial spokesman. Sir Frank Cooper delicately described the activities of this group as 'a touching hands exercise'.

Back to the MoD again, where McDonald would attend the daily meeting of the Chiefs of Staff committee. 'The higher you get,' declared Sir Terence Lewin, 'the more aware you are of the great importance of public support and the part that the media play in providing you with public support and parliamentary support.' The extent of that awareness was reflected in the prominence given to PR on the Chiefs of Staff Committee's agenda: it was always considered as the third item, after discussion of the relative military situations of Britain and Argentina. The Committee's members—the three service chiefs, Lewin, Cooper, Nott (or, more often, his private secretary), and representatives from the intelligence services and the Foreign Office—would listen while McDonald read out his summary of the editorial policies being adopted by each of the Fleet Street papers, devoting special attention to those critical of any aspects of the war. Drawing on the views of the Downing Street meeting, and having heard the latest information from the South Atlantic, McDonald would then outline what he thought should be released to the media. Almost every day, said Lewin, the committee would take a view on the content of the statement to be made at noon that day to the press and decide whether or not to release certain pieces of information.

McDonald would then personally clear his draft statement with Cooper and Nott. At about 11.45 it would be sent off for typing, while McDonald snatched a few moments to brief the senior members of his own PR department. Finally, at 12 o'clock McDonald would make his way to the Press Centre, read out the statement, and invite twenty minutes of questions, nearly all of which he would neatly sidestep. The journalists called these daily rituals 'The 12 o'clock Follies'.

McDonald sweetened these generally futile exchanges with an unexpected display of showmanship. He had mild eccentricities of pronunciation: like a good classicist, he insisted on calling *Hermes* 'Hermays'. He was always ready to deflect questions with a suitable quotation. When asked to comment on the reliability of Argentine claims, he referred the media to Act III, scene iv, lines 52–4 of *Hamlet*. A frantic search for a copy of the play revealed the information:

Look
Here, upon this picture, and on this,
The counterfeit presentment of two brothers.

When the press corps had a special information centre tie made—
a pattern of red question marks on a dark background—
McDonald took to wearing one. The atmosphere of camaraderie and
frustration, with anything up to 250 journalists milling around
waiting for news, reminded McDonald of a prisoner-of-war camp.

Little of the flavour of this was conveyed on television, for which
McDonald adopted an attitude of great solemnity. Most of his
statements were recorded and shown on news bulletins. Occasionally
he was cued in 'live'. McDonald had never appeared on camera
before. The only advice he was given beforehand was to hold his
hands still, to look straight ahead and to speak very slowly. The result
was so far removed from the normally slick performance of television
personalities as to make McDonald an overnight sensation. His slow
and mechanical delivery earned him the nickname 'McDalek' from
the press. To Keith Waterhouse he was 'the only man in the world
who speaks in Braille'. Richard Ingrams wrote: 'He looks and sounds
like some especially gloomy dean reading the second lesson at
Evensong in a huge and draughty cathedral.'

Television transformed McDonald from an unknown bureaucrat
into a national celebrity. Taxi drivers refused to take his fare. When it
became known that he was a bachelor, several offers of marriage
arrived at the MoD. Throughout the war, McDonald appeared to be
most popular with women viewers. One letter he still treasures reads
simply:

Ian McDonald MP,
Defence Minister.

Dear sir,
    I would like to thank you for the calm, soothing way you
handled every announcement during the Falklands conflict.
    As a mother of a marine who had serious burns out there, I can
say with confidence that YOU helped me and my family, so
don't let the stupid newspapers jibe you.
    And please stay in office. We need gentlemen like you.

Fleet Street printed every piece of information about him they could find: He was the son of a Glasgow fish merchant. He lived in Belsize Park. He was shy. He wore washable suits. He collected exotic Indian art. He enjoyed Shostakovitch and Emily Dickinson. He had a snowy-haired, 73-year-old mother. ('I've never known what he did at the Ministry of Defence,' she told Jean Rook of the *Daily Express*, 'until he suddenly appeared on the telly. He's a wonderful son to me....') A picture of McDonald aged six months was published, captioned 'The Naked Civil Servant'.

After the war, ITN attacked McDonald and recommended that 'In the event of a similar conflict, the chief defence spokesman should be a major military figure of the status of general or equivalent.' McDonald always argued strongly the other way: that by having all military information delivered by a civilian, Britain underlined that she was a democracy and 'scored a trick' over military dictatorships like Argentina. Besides, as he freely admitted, he was enjoying every moment of it.

But even as Ian McDonald was rising to prominence in newspaper articles and on television, his position behind the scenes was being undermined. Unknown to the media, a struggle was developing inside the MoD over who should control the Ministry's information policy.

Neville Taylor, the MoD's designated chief of public relations, had decided, in the light of the Falklands crisis, to leave the Department of Health and Social Security two months ahead of the originally agreed date in order to take up his new job at the Defence Ministry. He arrived on 13 April and immediately received an unpleasant surprise. When he opened his letter of appointment on his first morning he was informed that he was to take charge at once of all areas relating to the Ministry's public relations, *except the Falklands*. 'It merely said, in effect,' he recalled, '"You are chief of public relations. These are your responsibilities but for the time being you will not be responsible for the Falklands public relations activities."' He confessed to feeling 'some personal disapointment'.

This was scarcely surprising. Taylor, highly regarded by other senior Whitehall PR men, was a professional public relations expert. Until 1970 he had worked full-time at the MoD. He knew some of the service chiefs from the 1960s, when he had handled the media during the fighting in Indonesia. He chafed at his restricted responsibilities. 'I wanted to get stuck in the day I arrived,' he said. Instead he had to stand aside and watch a career civil servant doing the most important part of his job.

Given the natural antipathy that was likely to exist between two men who had competed for the same job only a few weeks before and the tremendous strain under which everyone at the senior levels in the MoD was working, a conflict between Taylor and McDonald became inevitable. Taylor came to represent all the grievances of the Ministry's professional public relations men who felt they had been by-passed by the administrator McDonald, who had centralized power in his own hands to a remarkable extent. All his staff had been forbidden to maintain their normal relations with the press. Only he was privy to the details of task-force operations through his attendance of the Chiefs of Staff Committee and his meetings with Cooper and Nott. He personally drafted the Ministry's public statements. Apart from rare occasions when a military expert was called in to provide additional information, only McDonald briefed the media.

The most frustrated group were the serving officers, the military directors of public relations whose normal task of looking after the 'image' of their particular services was completely suspended. Later Sir Terence Lewin was to express his sympathy with their predicament. 'I would have liked to have seen them playing a larger part earlier on,' he told the Commons Defence Committee, and went even further in his criticism:

> I believe not only could we have made more use of the Directors of Public Relations, Army, Navy and Air Force, who have built up a range of contacts with the media but also I believe we could have made more use of the public information officers, the public relations officers in each unit. Each unit in all the three services, down to ship, battalion, squadron level, has a nominated officer who as a part-time job is a public relations man . . . I do not think we made enough use of those chaps.

In retrospect, it was clearly one of the MoD's greatest failures. ITN 'repeatedly asked for facilities to record some of the efforts being carried out in industry, among the services and in the dockyards' but was turned down. 'To a public deprived of hard information about their own side and obliged to see and hear the uninhibited coverage of Argentine determination, such positive news would have come as water to a thirsty Bedouin.' As it was, 'great opportunities were missed for the positive projection of single-minded energy and determination by the British people in their support of the task force.' As David Nicholas shrewdly pointed out, the weeks during which there were no television pictures 'corresponded with the period when the Prime Minister was moved to ask why was nobody giving news about our boys'.

Another result of the concentration of power in the hands of McDonald was that the service PR directors—the DPRs—would often not learn what had been happening in the South Atlantic until fifteen minutes before McDonald gave out the information to the media gathered in the Press Centre. The nearest they came to any significant role was during the slack period in the afternoon, when, in the early days, McDonald would leave the MoD to snatch a few hours' rest. Then they each took a turn as acting chief of public relations on a rota basis.

To add insult to injury, the DPRs also had to face the anger of journalists demanding to know why no one in the MoD was any longer prepared to speak to them.

> Correspondents [wrote ITN] became aware of the tension between the press office machine and the military directors of public relations. The impression was that the DPRs were not privy to the fuller background enjoyed by the deputy chief press officer who had been briefed by the Permanent Under-Secretary.
>
> Tensions built up between the civil servants who were controlling the information, the military PR men, who thought they should be controlling it, and the poor 'desk officers', who knew little, said little, and received flak from the press corps.

'The information service was actually told less than the press were,' said Bob Hutchinson of PA. 'On many occasions we told the information service what was going on.' The BBC's Alan Protheroe, who maintains close contacts with the military PR men in the MoD, reflected their frustrations in an article in the *Listener*, describing how they had been 'discounted and virtually eliminated from full and proper participation by the "administrative" civil servants'; he added, in another dig at McDonald: 'This practised machine was shunted into a siding by the mandarins.'

Slowly at first, but with increasing determination, Taylor began to dismantle McDonald's control. His first direct involvement with the

Falklands war came towards the end of April, when he was put in overall charge of the arrangements for the establishment of the Emergency Press Centre. He also lobbied Sir Frank Cooper to restart the off-the-record briefings that had been stopped by McDonald at the beginning of the crisis.

Cooper had been surprised at the extent of the media's hostility, and later he came to believe that McDonald's plan had been a mistake. 'I think,' he told the House of Commons Defence Committee after the war, 'with hindsight, that was probably an unwise decision—that we should have gone on with them or restarted them rather more quickly than we did. I think, given one's time over again, I would not have done it that way, quite frankly.' He refused to accept that the cancellation of background briefings had added to the amount of speculation in the media, but conceded it had done nothing to stop it.

On 11 May Cooper held the first off-the-record briefing since McDonald imposed his ban. For the remainder of the war these were held twice a week, chaired by Cooper, usually accompanied by a senior military officer or civil servant.

As May wore on and the fighting in the South Atlantic escalated, the disagreements between McDonald and Taylor became more bitter. Taylor criticized what he felt was the rigidity of the arrangements by which McDonald handled the media. He also opposed the installation of permanent camera positions in the Press Centre on the grounds that the moment McDonald walked in, the lights were switched on and the most insignificant news was given an artificial sense of drama. For his part, McDonald wanted to increase the involvement of television. Often the noon statement was not read out but simply distributed as a printed press release. McDonald thought he should make a televised announcement every evening. There was, according to one witness, 'violent disagreement' over this, with Taylor insisting that it would make the Ministry of Defence totally synonymous in the public's mind with McDonald.

The most serious argument between the two men arose over censorship. Until the early part of May the only control over the dispatches of the task-force correspondents was exercised in the South Atlantic. But as the fleet moved further south and fighting began, this expedient came to be regarded as inadequate. Two incidents in particular provoked trouble in London. On 1 May, the Fleet's Commander-in-Chief, Admiral Sir John Fieldhouse, who was directing operations from the naval headquarters at Northwood, learned that the task force had shot down two Argentine Mirage fighters through watching the news on television. He promptly sent off an angry signal to *Hermes* demanding to know why he had not been informed first.

Two days later, a British submarine torpedoed the *General Belgrano*. Michael Nicholson, on board the MARISAT ship *Olmeda*, happened to overhear on the bridge the name of the nuclear submarine responsible, HMS *Conqueror*. This was confirmed to him by what he calls 'a senior naval source'. Nicholson promptly broadcast the information in a dispatch to ITN's *News at One*. As far as Fieldhouse was concerned, this was the final straw. Not only are the whereabouts of individual British submarines regarded as top secret, but the death toll inflicted by the *Conqueror* was so great that it was believed that the officers and crew should be shielded from adverse publicity. Fieldhouse fired off such a stinging rebuke to Captain Middleton on *Hermes* that Middleton, in order, as he put it, 'to make known to him my displeasure', never spoke to Nicholson again.

Fieldhouse demanded the setting up of a second screen of censorship in London to vet all copy dispatched from the task force. Individual captains were no longer to be trusted. 'It was my opinion that it should be taken out of their hands,' said the admiral, 'and that the overall control of information should be handled by the Ministry of Defence.'

The dispute between McDonald and Taylor was over the form which that censorship should take. McDonald thought that the media, as far as possible, should censor itself. He wanted to build on the D-Notice system of voluntary restraints by editors. It would, in his view, be courting disaster for the Ministry of Defence PR department to become involved in the vetting of copy. Once they started along such a path, it would lead inexorably to the accusation that they were censoring on the grounds of taste as much as for operational reasons. Taylor derided the ramshackle D-Notice system and put forward the view that if any group were going to operate a second tier of censorship, it would be better if it were PR experts who understood the demands of the media. Taylor won, and McDonald found himself adroitly outmanoeuvred and at odds with his own department's official policy.

It was at this point that Sir Frank Cooper intervened. His personal opinion was that McDonald had done a better job than his predecessor, but that Taylor would do a better job than McDonald. Having made a decision, Cooper, a formidable administrator, was not the kind of man to delay his implementation of it. ('He looks like a cuddly teddy bear,' says one of his colleagues, 'but he's deadly.') Towards the end of the second week in May, Cooper told McDonald that he thought he was in danger of overdoing it. He was looking tired and strained. He should take a holiday. McDonald demurred. Cooper insisted. On 14 May McDonald told reporters in the Press Centre that he was taking the weekend off to spend at home with his mother in Glasgow. When he returned to London three days later, he found that Neville Taylor was in complete control of the Ministry's PR department—including the Falklands. From 18 May onwards, McDonald was simply the Ministry's official spokesman.

By the middle of May, Sir Frank Cooper was conducting two regular sets of background briefings, one for editors, the other for defence correspondents. Neither was considered very useful.

The editors' meetings were concerned largely with complaints about facilities: it was soon apparent that they had nothing to do with information. On one occasion, 6 May, Sir Frank Cooper kept silent about the loss of two Harriers in a mid-air collision, while downstairs in the Press Centre it had become common knowledge and was shortly afterwards announced by Ian McDonald. Brian Hitchen of the *Daily Star* described the meetings as 'farcical':

> I was originally under the impression that the reason for the briefings was to establish mutual trust and understanding between the MoD and the press so that certain information which the Chiefs of Staff may not have wanted held up to the public eye could be discussed and explained. This was a naive dream on the part of myself and most editors.

The *Observer* described them as 'mostly unproductive'. Occasionally they degenerated into noisy squabbles; Derek Jameson in particular was vociferous in his attacks on Sir Frank. 'Whenever it got a bit hot,' says Jameson, 'he'd drag up "the national interest". Here are you screaming, "Where's my bloody pictures?" and he says "It's my job to safeguard lives." There's not much of an answer to that.' At one meeting a television executive told Cooper that the MoD's organization of press coverage 'isn't a cock-up. It's an effing cock-up.'

Jameson joined in asking: 'Next time, why don't you borrow the Israeli army's director of public relations?' 'Cooper', says Hitchen, 'slammed down his glass of water, gathered up his papers and said, "I don't have to take this." We were all left looking at one another.' It was at one of these sessions that William Deedes, editor of the *Daily Telegraph* and an old friend of Cooper's, presented the Permanent Under-Secretary with a copy of *Scoop* and referred him to the passage in which the foreign correspondents—'all, in their various tongues, voluble with indignation'—confront the Minister of Propaganda.

The defence correspondents proved to be much better behaved. Only 'accredited' journalists—that is, reporters recognized by the MoD as established defence writers, representing 'reputable' publications—were admitted to Cooper's meetings. When the *Sunday People*, which doesn't have a defence correspondent, hastily appointed one, he wasn't considered to be in the 'front line' and received less access to briefings than his colleagues. Second-class treatment was also given to the Scottish, foreign and provincial press. The men at Cooper's briefings were all journalists well known to the MoD, reporters used to Whitehall's 'lobby' system, in which politicians and civil servants give briefings attributable only to a 'senior source'. The dangers of the lobby, its tendency to corrupt journalists and to leave them vulnerable to manipulation, have often been pointed out. As David Leigh wrote in his book on the press and government, *The Frontiers of Secrecy*: 'Having had their hands tied, journalists in Britain are then made to dance.' When the MoD's non-attributable briefings were stopped by Ian McDonald at the beginning of the war, many reporters were left gasping for information, like patients whose life-support systems had been switched off. Now that 'background' material was flowing again, the journalists were grateful—and ripe targets for misinformation.

The most dangerous moment of the war, as far as the British were concerned, was the landing on the Falklands. 'I think getting people ashore,' said Cooper later, 'and even more important, getting the supplies that go with the people ashore so that they can survive ... was perhaps the most sensitive part of the whole operation.' The key to the task force's strategy was to take the Argentines by surprise, make an unopposed landing, and consolidate as rapidly as possible. An amphibious assault is one of the most hazardous of military ventures, in which all the advantages lie with the defender. When the Allies landed in France in June 1944, the real operation, 'Overlord', was covered by a deception plan ('Fortitude') designed to convince the Germans that the main attack would not be in Normandy. No 'Fortitude'-style deception was planned for the Falklands. But anything which might confuse the Argentines would help to ensure the success of the British landings.

At the morning meeting of the Chiefs of Staff on Thursday, 20 May, the committee held a final discussion on the task force's plan to put 3,000 men ashore at San Carlos Bay. Although it was agreed that Admiral Woodward could alter the timing of the assault at his discretion, it was provisionally fixed for 4 a.m. on Friday morning.

Twelve hours before the landings, at 4 p.m. on Thursday afternoon, Cooper met the defence correspondents. 'I have looked up my notes that I made at that briefing,' Jim Meacham told MPs in July.

> We were told that there were all sorts of things going on all over the islands—I think that is the correct quote—which we took to mean various little raids. We were told that we could expect to see more of these small raids along the lines of Pebble Island [which had occurred a week earlier, when eleven Argentine aircraft were destroyed] but not to expect a D-Day landing. . . .

The briefing only lasted fifteen minutes, and at the end of it the correspondents dutifully filed out to report what they had been told.

The Fleet Street press the following morning was unanimous in its descriptions of Britain's next military move. Both the *Daily Mirror* and the *Daily Express* had the same front page headline: 'SMASH AND GRAB'. According to the *Mirror*:

> There will be no bloody D-Day style landings. Instead the 5,000 troops who have been prepared for action for days will begin a series of attacks by air and sea.

The *Express* claimed:

> There will be no mass landing, D-Day style. It will be a series of smash-and-grab operations by the back door, knocking out the Argentinian occupation bit by bit. . . . The defence source said: 'There will *not* be a single punch.'

The *Daily Telegraph* reported:

> a single D-Day type frontal assault has been ruled out. . . .

'Attrition is the name of the game,' said a senior Whitehall source . . . . there [will] be no set-piece battle.'

The *Guardian* quoted 'highly placed Whitehall sources':

Rear Admiral Sandy Woodward is about to begin a series of landings and hit-and-run raids against Argentine positions on the islands. . . . There [will] not be a D-Day type invasion.

The Times wrote:

Sources were not expecting to see a repeat performance of D-Day.

And the *Sun* declared:

It means a series of hit-and-run raids, not a massive invasion. Whitehall chiefs predicted a war of attrition . . . . they ruled out a huge single operation like D-Day. . . .

In the early hours of Friday morning, as Fleet Street papers bearing this unanimous message were distributed around the country, 3,000 troops were going ashore on the Falklands in Britain's biggest amphibious assault since D-Day. The briefing had been totally misleading, but Cooper was unrepentant. He told the Commons Defence Committee:

When I saw the press on the evening before, I certainly did not tell them the whole story. I make no bones about that whatsoever. I certainly said I did not expect a D-Day type of invasion, and I did not expect a D-Day type of invasion because the whole aim of the operation was to get the forces ashore on an unopposed landing. A D-Day type invasion in my mind is actually an opposed landing—and, if I may say so, I knew what I was talking about because I have been on one—but I certainly did not tell people that we were going ashore with the forces that we were. I am quite ready to accept that I did not unveil the whole picture, and I am delighted there was a good deal of speculation, and it was very helpful to us, quite frankly. . . . We did not tell a lie—but we did not tell the whole truth.

Cooper's suggestion that in ruling out a D-Day landing he was actually only ruling out an opposed landing is a flimsy excuse. 'I personally reject this disingenuous explanation. Every journalist in that room had the same impression I did at that briefing,' says Meacham. 'It certainly gave me the impression that we were not going to see a main landing and we did see one. There is no question in my mind whatsoever that that was done on purpose.' The unanimity of the press coverage, the use even of the same phrases, suggests that Cooper's message to the journalists was quite clear: there would be no single, large-scale assault, opposed or unopposed; there would instead be a war of attrition.

If Cooper did deliberately mislead the press—and his defence is more a matter of nuance than outright denial—was he justified? Immediately before the briefing he spoke to Ian McDonald about what he intended to say and told him: 'You really don't understand how vulnerable we are.' Later he described the British military situation as critical: 'We were really right at the end of the string.' When the task force commanders returned to London and met Cooper after the recapture of the Falklands, they all shared one reaction: immense relief that they had been able to carry out an unopposed landing. Cooper had reason to believe that British newspapers were closely monitored in Argentina. If the deliberate planting of false stories could mislead the enemy for a crucial twenty-four hours while the bridgehead was established, why not do it?

The implications of a policy of misinformation for a democracy reliant on a free press are immense. But even putting those issues to one side for the moment, there is the obvious, practical danger that the long-term damage of such a policy will far outweigh any short-term benefits. By the end of the Falklands war, the Ministry of Defence was fast losing credibility, even among journalists normally sympathetic to it. 'I still find myself now,' says Bob Hutchinson, defence correspondent of the Press Association, 'months after the Falklands, speaking to the Ministry of Defence over quite trivial things and not actually believing what they say, because the seven weeks inside the Ministry of Defence taught me not to believe what they say.' Incidents of misinformation like those concerning HMS *Superb*, the recapture of South Georgia and the San Carlos landings did lasting damage to press relations and to the image of Britain abroad. 'Those briefings may have had the effect of misleading the Argentine forces,' wrote the editor-in-chief of Reuters. 'They certainly had the effect of reducing the credibility in many countries of British Government statements we reported thereafter.' Michael Evans, defence correspondent of the *Daily Express*, found that after

20 May MoD statements were 'treated with considerably more scepticism'. The *Observer* wrote that 'the net result of such misinformation was greatly to erode our confidence in the reliability of MoD briefings as a useful source of information.' Politicians, civil servants, and military commanders will hardly be in a position to complain in the future if the media reports enemy claims as well as our own and refuses to accept at face value everything issued by the British authorities: the Falklands war undermined the assumption that it is the other side which always lies and never the British.

Five days after Cooper's briefing, on Tuesday, 25 May, the MoD's information policy came under attack once more. At 8.30 p.m. that evening, ITN were setting up their equipment in John Nott's office to record an interview for that night's *News at Ten*. Nott arrived on time, but just as he was about to sit down, a sheaf of signals was thrust into his hand. He thumbed through them with increasing dismay. They informed him (erroneously, as it later turned out) that a number of ships had been hit during Argentine air attacks and that the situation was serious. Nott told the ITN team that he would have to pull out of the interview. The journalists could see that something was wrong. Nott blurted out that the MoD 'had some news' and that he would try to give them a live interview at 10 p.m.

A short while later, Fleet Headquarters at Northwood received a signal from the South Atlantic stating that HMS *Coventry*, a Type 42 destroyer, had been hit, and that she had capsized and sunk within twenty minutes. It was, says one senior MoD official, 'a hideous evening'. The First Sea Lord told Nott that as the ship had sunk so quickly, she might well have taken most of her 280 crew with her.

The immediate reaction of the Navy was to keep the whole episode secret. As Sir Henry Leach explained, *Coventry* had been fitted with the Sea Dart missile system. 'The Argentinians had Sea Dart and there is no doubt that the nature of their air attacks was constrained by their knowledge of Sea Dart.' The news that, after *Sheffield*, a second ship fitted with the system had also been knocked out, 'could have affected their immediate operations'.

From Northwood, Sir John Fieldhouse rang Sir Terence Lewin and asked him to ensure that the media heard nothing: he wanted to avoid letting Argentina know about the loss of the ship, and also to have time to contact the next of kin of the men killed. Lewin was forced to tell him that such a policy was impossible: Nott had already hinted at bad news to ITN, and rumours were by now spreading downstairs through the Press Centre.

Nott intended to appear on *News at Ten* and wanted to announce that *Coventry* had been hit. The senior naval men were horrified. Lewin and Leach, with Fieldhouse joining in by telephone, strongly urged Nott to say nothing. Lewin said later: 'We were unanimous and said, "Don't announce it." The Secretary of State wanted to announce the name of the ship but accepted our military advice.' The compromise agreed was that Nott should announce that one ship had been hit, but that he would not name her.

Nott had to leave immediately for the ITN studios in Wells Street, near Oxford Circus. As he walked out of the Ministry of Defence, he told Ian McDonald to make an announcement in the Press Centre simultaneously with his interview on ITN. Nott said he would work out the form of words he would use while being driven to the studio in his car. His private secretary would ring McDonald when they arrived at ITN and dictate to him the statement he should read.

The audience which watched Nott that night was later estimated to be 10.2 million. He said that 'bad news' had been received: 'One of our ships has been badly damaged and she's in difficulties. I can't give any further details at the moment—the news is still coming in about her. Clearly, from what we know at the moment it is bad news, and I should say that right away.'

It was a serious misjudgement. In the remoteness of the television studio, Nott had no idea of the effect his words were having. In the crowded atmosphere of the Press Centre, Ian McDonald knew at once that they had made a mistake in not announcing *Coventry*'s name. The mood of the journalists was so sombre that having read the statement, McDonald, on his own initiative, told the reporters that the ship 'in difficulties' was not one of the aircraft carriers. When the journalists began pressing him, and asked whether it was the *Canberra*, he turned on his heel and walked out of the room.

In their anxiety to preserve security, the naval commanders caused widespread anxiety throughout the country. Leach said that relatives of 'the entire task force rang up that night' to ask for news. Fleet Street newspapers described themselves as 'besieged' with calls and Mike Molloy attacked Nott's method of breaking the news while at the same time leaving the country in suspense as 'deplorable and heavy-handed'. 'If after last night's news I had had a relative with the task force,' said the BBC's Richard Francis, 'I would have had a most terrible night. I am very worried that this whole thing has not been thought through.'

'It was quite obvious by next morning we were wrong,' admitted Lewin, 'but it was a decision that was made in a very short time and under great pressure.'

The *Coventry* affair added fresh voices to the chorus of complaints against the MoD. Peter Viggers, the Conservative MP for Gosport, had been watching *News at Ten* with some servicemen's wives . 'They have been worried all night,' he said on 26 May. 'All they heard yesterday was that a ship had been damaged, but they didn't know which ship it was.' That afternoon in the House of Commons John Nott agreed with MPs that 'in retrospect' withholding *Coventry's* name 'may have been the wrong judgement'. Privately he was angry at having allowed his instincts to be overruled by the military, and he pointedly told MPs that he had been 'relying very much on the advice of the Chief of the Defence Staff and the Chief of the Naval Staff, and, through them, the Commander-in-Chief'.

One of the most persistent critics of the MoD's handling of press and public relations was the chief press secretary at 10 Downing Street, Bernard Ingham. At the beginning of the war he had been astonished at Ian McDonald's decision to suspend normal relations with the media. 'I certainly took the view that when you are in a crisis of this kind, the last thing you do is withdraw the service to the media,' he said later. 'I think that is not the time to withdraw your service to your clientele.' Ingham expressed his views bluntly to McDonald and lobbied hard to have Neville Taylor installed as chief of public relations.

'We got the distinct impression,' said Bob Hutchinson, 'that Number 10 was more than unhappy at the way the MoD were handling the war—*more* than unhappy—and there were times when Number 10 were briefing on subjects which the MoD refused to talk about.'

Downing Street was more alert than the Ministry to the need to maintain good relations with the press—'to keep them sweet and on our side', as McDonald put it. Just as the MoD used the media to confuse the enemy, so Ingham and the rest of the Government sought to use them to sustain public support for the war.

In the week that *Coventry* was lost, the press were encouraged by political sources to believe that the British forces were about to move out from their bridgehead at San Carlos Bay. 'We are planning to move and to move fast,' Cecil Parkinson assured radio listeners on Sunday, 23 May. 'It is not our intention to be drawn into a long and bloody war.' That afternoon, Ingham briefed journalists in similar terms, and Fleet Street the following day painted a morale-boosting picture of the British land forces poised to strike. 'We're not going to fiddle around,' Ingham—disguised as 'a senior source'—was quoted as saying.

As Sir Frank Cooper later pointed out, there were few strategic options open to the British land forces. Assured all week by official statements that an attack was imminent, journalists studied their maps of the Falklands and concluded that the British were about to move south from the bridgehead to attack Darwin and Goose Green. Speculation was further encouraged by a forty-eight-hour blackout on news from the Falklands. The *Daily Express*, which had predicted an attack following Ingham's briefing at the beginning of the week, gave over its front page on 27 May to a wildly inaccurate story actually headlined 'GOOSE GREEN IS TAKEN'. Speculation was boosted by Mrs Thatcher during Prime Minister's Questions. 'Our forces on the ground,' she told MPs amid murmurs of approval, 'are now moving forward from the bridgehead.' On the same day, John Nott told a private meeting of backbenchers to 'expect good news'.

Unaware of this excitement in London, 8,000 miles away on the Falklands men of the 2nd Parachute Regiment were moving in to position for their assault on 27 May when they heard a BBC defence correspondent broadcast over the World Service that they were about to attack Goose Green. In Bush House, after five days of officially inspired anticipation, the report seemed harmless enough. But to many of the soldiers it looked as if their plans had been leaked behind their backs in London. 'How many enemies are we supposed to be fighting?' asked one man. Max Hastings reported: 'The colonel commanding the positions attacked by Skyhawks last night told me furiously that if a BBC correspondent arrived in his area, he would be sent immediately to the prisoner-of-war cage.' Colonel 'H' Jones, commander of the paratroops, muttered savage threats of suing 'John Nott, the Ministry, the Prime Minister, if anyone's killed'.

In the event, eighteen men, including Jones himself, died in the attack, and there was a controversy in London. The World Service held its own inquest into the affair, and the BBC issued a statement insisting that it had broadcast 'no information which has not been readily available to other broadcasters and other journalistic organizations from official sources in London, *including the MoD'*. Stung by this, and by Jones's widely reported intention of suing him, John Nott ordered a detailed investigation within the Ministry of Defence. An internal report blamed general speculation and failed to trace any specific leak within the Ministry. But coming so soon after the public relations blunder over HMS *Coventry*, the incident did the MoD damage. Its credibility was not enhanced by the fact that, following a misinterpreted telephone call from the Falklands, it had announced the recapture of Darwin and Goose Green at 9.40 p.m. on Friday, 28 May—eighteen hours before the Argentine garrison surrendered.

Reporters who detected a division between the MoD and Number 10 had their suspicions confirmed eleven days later. On 8 June, enemy aircraft attacked the landing ships *Sir Galahad* and *Sir Tristram* at Bluff Cove. Fifty men were killed. 'We wished to conceal the extent of the casualties,' said Sir Terence Lewin, 'because we knew from intelligence that the Argentines thought they were very much higher.'

For three days, on the orders of John Nott and the Chiefs of Staff, the Ministry of Defence refused to release the number of casualties. 'There were deliberate attempts to get the media to exaggerate the numbers of dead and wounded,' claimed the Press Association. 'Reports of 220 dead and more than 400 wounded emanated from a radio ham in the Falklands, doubtless briefed by the military, and picked up in Bristol.'

On 10 June, Nott refused to disclose the extent of British losses to the House of Commons. Later that same day he had a meeting with journalists who pressed him for guidance on the number of casualties. He told them: 'Speculate as you wish.' 'The Bluff Cove incident,' admitted Lewin, 'when we deliberately concealed the casualty figures, was an example of using the press, the media, to further our military operations.'

By Friday, 11 June, Ingham thought the speculation had been allowed to go on long enough. The *Sun* appeared that morning with a banner headline stating '70 DEAD'. Ingham told correspondents that he believed the number of casualties was less than that figure. The MoD was furious: the Downing Street briefing, said Neville Taylor, 'became the subject of pretty heated discussion between Bernard Ingham and myself'.

By the end of the war, the Ministry of Defence's reputation for telling the truth had fallen so low in the estimation of the media that rumours began circulating that 'psyops'—military jargon for psychological warfare operations—were being conducted against the press.

It was known that one psyops unit was operating within the MoD. This was the team which ran the British propaganda station, Radio Atlantico del Sur, designed to lower the morale of Argentine troops on the Falklands. A BBC transmitter was requisitioned, and from 19 May onwards it broadcast a stream of pro-British news stories, sentimental music, appeals for peace and lists of Argentine wounded. Interrogation reports from captured troops were used to enable 'record requests' to be played for individual Argentinians on the islands, such as Captain Malinotti, 'all the boys from Santa Fé' and Colonel de Rega . . . .

The Press Association was told that psyops were also used to misinform the British media. 'Apparently two lieutenant-colonels and a wing-commander from the Latimer Defence College were brought to the Ministry to develop psyops themes. Initially there was, we reliably understand, an attempt to mix this input with information coming out of the Ministry.' A senior MoD official privately cites two stories he claims were planted by psyops personnel. One was a graphic but fictitious account of the activities of the Special Boat Section in the recapture of South Georgia, which found its way into at least one newspaper. The second—which the MoD information department refused to release—came from one of the ships with the task force, and reported that after his plane had been hit, an Argentinian pilot had baled out and landed *astride* one of their guns.

Psyops was added to the catalogue of complaints against the MoD: a list of grievances so long, loudly expressed and detailed that four days before the end of the war, the House of Commons Defence Committee announced its intention of investigating the Ministry's handling of press and public information during the Falklands crisis. Their inquiries were to cover not merely the allegations against the MoD in London, but also the growing volume of criticism filtering back from the South Atlantic.

7. From Our Own Correspondent

As *Canberra* neared the Falklands, the journalists on board underwent an intensive series of briefings to prepare them for the land campaign ahead. There were demonstrations in first aid and lectures on such minutiae of survival as how to catch and eat sea birds. Patrick Bishop of the *Observer* wrote:

> We were taught how to build stone sangars out of rocks and peat to protect ourselves from shell splinters and enemy bombs; how to dig slit trenches and shell scrapes to increase our chances of coming through a bombardment alive; and the importance of having 18 inches of dirt above your head to stop the shrapnel from airburst bombs.

The *Canberra* journalists consoled themselves with the knowledge that they were at last about to get ahead of their rivals on *Hermes* and *Invincible*. For more than a month they had been complaining to the Ministry of Defence minders that the reporters with the carrier group were stealing all the glory: they had been able to file first-hand reports of the Harrier attack on Port Stanley, the loss of *Sheffield*, the sea and air bombardment of the Falklands, the attack on Pebble Island, as well as on numerous sorties and air raids. The *Canberra* journalists had been under some pressure from their offices for equally good stories. Kim Sabido had actually been asked by Independent Radio News to read out a report on the recapture of South Georgia implying that *Canberra* was involved in it, even though he was hundreds of miles away from the island and had only heard about it on the World Service.

As a result of the *Canberra* press corps' complaints, the task force commanders had decided, shortly after leaving Ascension Island, to give them an advantage in the land campaign by allowing them to go ashore on the Falklands first. 'They had not had anything to report at that time,' said General Moore. 'I believe there was a feeling . . . that it was their turn and they should be allowed to go and get their bit of coverage, whereas the other people who had been reporting on what had been going on at sea had had their show for the moment. . . .'

Each *Canberra* journalist was attached to a unit. Bishop, for example, was assigned to cover 42 Commando; Robert Fox and David Norris to 2 Para; Alastair McQueen, Max Hastings and Jeremy Hands to 40 Commando. Robert McGowan of the *Daily Express* joined 3 Para: 'I spent a lot of time with them. They briefed me on how to survive, the sort of clothing I would need which they supplied, the sort of terrain, the weather, the kind of food I would be eating and the kind of opposition they thought we would be up against.' A couple of days before the landings, most of the journalists transferred with their units to the landing ships *Intrepid* and *Fearless* and prepared to go ashore.

Meanwhile on the aircraft carriers things were not running so smoothly. On *Hermes* Captain Middleton had by now been refusing to speak to Michael Nicholson for two and a half weeks. The tensions on the flagship which had existed on the voyage to Ascension had worsened. On 11 May, Admiral Woodward was told by the MoD that a Nicholson dispatch had alerted the Argentines to the fact that the carrier group was moving inshore to carry out a naval bombardment. 'I said nothing of the sort,' complained Nicholson in his diary, 'but Woodward says he has asked for a transcript ex London and I'll be "sacked" if it's true. Transcript confirms I said nothing of the kind. No apology.'

> It was at this time [wrote Nicholson] we decided, because of the continuing hassle, that we should prefix our reports 'Censored'. But we were told by MoD PR Graham Hammond and the Navy that this wouldn't be allowed. Peter Archer of the Press Association sent a service telex to his London boss saying his reports were censored. The word 'censored' was censored.
>
> I find it extraordinary that when BBC/ITN men in Poland sent censored reports out of that country in the days post-martial law, Polish censorship was made public. When I sent back censored reports years ago from Israel and Pakistan again I said so. We aboard *Hermes* were not allowed to make British censorship public.

On 15 May Nicholson witnessed the attack on Pebble Island from

HMS *Glamorgan* but was unable to get off in time to file a story that night. 'I confronted [the] lieutenant in charge of helicopter assets. I was told, "You bastards are the lowest-priority rating, at the bottom of the list, and that's where you'll remain."' Peter Archer wrote;

> Early one evening I handed copy to the *Hermes* MOD man who was sitting in the wardroom drinking a glass of port. I told him the story was urgent and asked if it could be dealt with immediately. I returned half an hour later to find the unvetted copy soaking up port and other spilt liquors on a wardroom table.

The constant air attacks, worry about his family and the frustrations of trying to report what was happening eventually proved too much for Archer. He wanted to leave. It was arranged between the Ministry of Defence and the Press Association editor in London that he should return home, and Archer was on his way back within twenty-four hours. His replacement, Richard Savill, was flown to Ascension and joined HMS *Bristol*. He was preceded by a characteristic signal sent by Sir John Fieldhouse warning the task force to be careful of him:

> HMS *Bristol* personnel to avoid discussion of any operational matters with Savill, who can be expected to take full advantage of his environment to glean newsworthy information. Speculation on possible courses of action, operational capability of task force/individual units and state of readiness must also be avoided. Names of ships and individual units should not be specified. . . .

The tensions on the other aircraft carrier HMS *Invincible* had been building up ever since the carrier had left Ascension. 'Anxiety was running very high,' recalls Gareth Parry. 'We were spending up to fourteen hours a day at defence stations, sweating out air alerts in anti-flash suits. In a situation like that you get tired and irritable.'

The physical discomfort heightened the feeling of professional frustration. Although, as the *Canberra* journalists had pointed out, the reporters on *Hermes* and *Invincible* were in the thick of the action, they were generally not allowed to report on anything that had happened until after it had been announced in London. The journalists on the two carriers would be told that a news blackout had been imposed on such incidents as the Vulcan bomber attack on Port Stanley, the destruction of HMS *Sheffield*, the loss of two Harriers in a mid-air collision—only to hear the same news announced over the BBC World Service a few hours later. By the time the *Invincible* journalists filed their reports, they were out of date. 'All our major news stories arrived too late for publication,' claimed Tony Snow. 'The common feeling among journalists with the task force was that we were risking our lives for nothing.'

Captain Jeremy Black was sympathetic to the newsmen's feelings, and on 7 May he signalled London with a proposal that journalists' copy should be transmitted from the task force as quickly as possible and then held in London for simultaneous release with the Ministry of Defence's official announcement. He never received a reply.

Although he tried to be helpful, Black was in fact losing patience with the five journalists on *Invincible*. A series of incidents, trivial in themselves but cumulative in their effects, gradually transformed him from one of the few naval officers who were happy to talk to the press to a man who couldn't wait to get them off his ship.

On 6 May, Mick Seamark wrote a story beginning 'Day Thirty-Two: Death Stares Us in the Face', which prompted Black to call the correspondents together and lecture them on the need to avoid damaging the morale of families at home. The next day, following the mid-air collision of two Harriers, Black had to deal with a complaint from the squadron's commanding officer, 'Sharky' Ward, that he had been 'doorstepped' that morning outside his cabin by Snow and Seamark demanding an interview about the missing pilots.

An indication of Black's shortening temper came on 13 May, when he learned that Michael Nicholson had come on board to interview survivors from the Argentine fishing vessel *Narval*. He gave Roger Goodwin, the MoD minder, a 'very uncomfortable five minutes', demanding to know how Nicholson had got on *Invincible* despite the fact that he had issued orders a month ago that he was never to set foot on board again.

On 15 May he once more called Goodwin in to see him, this time to tell him that the press's dispatches on the Pebble Island raid, submitted that evening, were much too long and detailed to be transmitted. Goodwin decided to wake Alfred McIlroy of the *Daily Telegraph* at 1.30 a.m., and between them the two men set about drastically cutting the entire press's copy. The atmosphere the next day when this was discovered was described by Goodwin as 'frosty'.

Three days later there was more trouble when one journalist used the MARISAT link on *Olmeda* to call his girlfriend, causing great resentment among crewmen, all of whom had been forbidden to make personal calls.

The crisis in relations between Black and the press came to a head on 19 May, when Black went on the ship's closed-circuit television to announce that the landings were to take place at San Carlos Bay the day after next. Several journalists took notes from the briefing, which were immediately confiscated by one of Black's naval secretaries. Then Alfred McIlroy tried to send a message to his office: 'Please close my New York bank account as there is only a dollar left'—which Black suspected of being a coded reference to the landings. Black was now keen to get rid of the press. For their part, the journalists were anxious to escape from the claustrophobic atmosphere of the ship and to cover the imminent landings.

They had no suitable clothing. They had no equipment. They had no rations. They had not been given any training. They had no units to join when they did get on shore. Nevertheless, Black and Goodwin decided that the reporters should leave *Invincible*—which was not going inshore—and that Goodwin would then attempt to persuade the army to accept them on land.

On 20 May, a grey day with high winds lashing the ships with rain, *Invincible* rendezvoused with the Royal Fleet Auxiliary *Resource*. The *Invincible* journalists, together with Goodwin, left the carrier by helicopter and were winched down on to the deck of the *Resource*. To the correspondents' dismay, they discovered that they were on an ammunition ship, heavily laden with bullets, shells, grenades and anti-aircraft missiles, and that they would not be moving into San Carlos Bay until at least two days after the landings. In addition, the reporters were told that the ship's MARISAT system had broken down. For the next two days the *Resource* stayed out at sea with the carrier group. When the MARISAT was repaired, the five journalists filed stories on the landings based on what they heard over the World Service and any scraps of information they could pick up on board.

On 23 May, the *Resource* moved to join *Canberra*, and Goodwin journeyed over to the liner to discuss the predicament of the 'Invincible Five', as they had become known, with the chief Ministry of Defence press officer, Martin Helm. He was told that the plan was for them to wait and join 5 Brigade, at that moment heading southwards on board the *Queen Elizabeth II*. When Goodwin returned to *Resource* and told the reporters the arrangement, he met with a barrage of abuse and complaints. As if to emphasize their lack of preparation, the 'Invincible Five' were joined by three *Canberra* reporters, Kim Sabido, Patrick Bishop and John Shirley, who had just filed stories on the landings and were returning to shore. 'They were all dressed up like action men,' says Parry. 'They'd got morphine jabs and field dressings, proper boots, waterproofs, helmets and sleeping bags. We felt pretty sick.'

That night, under cover of darkness, *Resource* moved into San Carlos Bay. At dawn on 24 May, the reporters woke up to find themselves a few hundred yards from shore. It was the *Invincible* journalists' first glimpse of the Falklands.

The Argentine air attacks began at midday. Parry innocently inquired why no one was wearing anti-flash gear. 'Because,' came the reply, 'if we get hit, what you'll need is a fucking parachute.' Parry was told that *Resource* was carrying explosives equivalent to half the force of the Hiroshima atom bomb. When the air raids began, Sabido was down below. 'I ran up on to the deck. I looked around, and there, coming in at head-height, was an Argentine plane. I could literally see the pilot's face as he flashed past.' A photograph taken from on board *Resource* that day shows the *Stromness* less than 100 yards away and between the two ships a massive fountain of water where a bomb has just exploded. Some journalists took shelter in the bowels of the ship. Parry stayed on deck: 'At least you can see what's going on out in the open. It's considered bad for morale to sound an air-raid warning on an ammunition ship, so the only way you could tell when they were coming in again was to catch the noise of alerts drifting across the bay from other ships.'

That afternoon, the 'Invincible Five' suffered the anguish of watching the three fully equipped journalists from *Canberra* clambering on board a helicopter and being flown the quarter of a mile to rejoin their units on land.

Some sort of solution was clearly becoming urgent. Goodwin—who had spent the air raids pressed face-down on the deck—had received a message from Brigade Headquarters on shore telling him that the five reporters would be offered a 'facility ashore once situation stabilized'. That could take days. Goodwin went across to *Fearless* and made contact with a naval lieutenant who promised to try to arrange for the journalists to be taken ashore. The next morning—now four days after the landings—Goodwin took a unilateral decision to get his press contingent off *Resource*, whether the land forces were ready for them or not.

It was a decision warmly welcomed by the press. As Gareth Parry later told the Commons Defence Committee: 'Four days on a fully laden ammunition ship under air attack almost by the hour is enough to prompt you into a good idea of where you should be and where you should not be and—I am not being facetious—it really is the wrong place to be.'

Goodwin's reasoning was that the marines would simply have to accept the presence of the reporters as a *fait accompli*. He ushered four of them—Gareth Parry, Tony Snow, Mick Seamark and John Witherow—into a helicopter and watched, with a feeling of great relief, as they disappeared towards the shore. (McIlroy stayed at sea for a few more hours that afternoon and left in the early evening.)

'It felt marvellous to be ashore,' remembers Parry. 'Especially the silence. All we'd had for seven weeks was noise. The peace was beautiful. You could drink it. And the natural colours, the greens, something completely absent at sea.' The tranquillity lasted only a short time. The helicopter pilot had deposited them in a muddy field full of sheep, miles away from Brigade Headquarters where they were supposed to be. There was nothing to do but walk. Parry recalled:

> The day ended with a march in total darkness along what appeared to be a succession of country lanes. It was pitch-black. The hedges along either side were filled with snipers. Every so often as you went along you'd hear a bush rattle its bolt. We were terrified. We could have been shot at any moment. Added to which, we soon realized we were following an escort who didn't know where Brigade HQ actually was.

Alan Percival, an MoD minder from *Canberra*, was sitting in a potting shed close to Brigade HQ checking reporters' copy, when, shortly after 7 p.m., the door opened and Alfred McIlroy appeared. McIlroy had been dropped by helicopter in the *right* location. He had no sleeping bag and was wearing an ordinary pair of shoes. He asked Percival for some kit. Percival told him there wasn't any: any spare equipment had been given to the medical teams and crews manning the Rapier missile batteries. Brigadier Julian Thompson had informed Percival that he hadn't so much as a single pair of windproof trousers to give to the journalists. Percival told McIlroy he would have to leave. Even fully equipped marines and paratroopers were being evacuated, suffering from exposure. McIlroy left under protest, telling Percival he would write a story announcing that he'd been thrown off the Falklands by the British Army.

Finally, at midnight, the potting shed door opened again to admit Parry, Witherow, Seamark and Snow. They, too, had expected to find extra equipment and at first refused to believe that there were no spare sets of clothing in the entire task force. All Parry had managed to cobble together before leaving *Invincible* were 'bits and pieces, webbing that did not fit and a pack with no handles which was next to useless'. They had lightweight navy boots, but these were little protection in the freezing weather and thick mud. Percival told them they would not be accepted by any unit and they would have to leave at first light.

The four journalists spent the night in a nearby house, huddled for warmth between the sleeping bags of some arctic warfare troops, and agreed the following morning between themselves to try to avoid being sent back—especially if it meant going back to an ammunition ship. They went and hid among some bales of wool.

An hour or so later, they were spotted by Kim Sabido.

> John Shirley, Patrick Bishop and myself were walking by when we saw the four *Invincible* journalists all hiding, wearing Navy boiler suits and carrying what looked like a suitcase. It was pathetic. The only rations they had was a packet of cheese sandwiches they'd been given by the ship's cook on *Resource*. We asked them what they were doing. They said they were hiding and begged us not to give them away.

'We were actually under air attack at the time,' says Parry. 'I was sheltering in a crevice. One of the *Canberra* journalists said, "My God, am I pissed off to see you. You guys have got no right to be here." I thought: what a welcome. We would have been delighted to have shared the Exocet attacks with them.' To this day, Parry believes they were 'betrayed' by one of the *Canberra* reporters. The four *Invincible* men were rounded up by Alan Percival, together with a Royal Marine public relations officer, Captain David Nicholls, and put on board the landing ship, *Sir Geraint*, where they were joined by Alfred McIlroy. The empty ship, which had no MARISAT link, sailed back out into the Total Exclusion Zone which the reporters had left six days before. There it patrolled endlessly up and down in front of the carriers. At first the journalists were unable to work out what was happening. Then they realized that they were on board an Exocet decoy, designed to draw off a missile attack from the big ships.

The representatives of all three British 'quality' daily newspapers, together with reporters from two mass-circulation tabloids, spent the next eight days stranded out at sea, filing occasional stories based on reports heard over the World Service. On 31 May, the fifth day in this captivity, Gareth Parry recorded laconically in his diary: 'Still waiting in the Total Exclusion Zone. Bright clear day. Perfect missile-attack weather. Yesterday we learned two missiles were launched against us. But apparently they missed.' It was about this time that Parry began receiving signals from the Ministry of Defence addressed to 'Paul Keel', a *Guardian* reporter working in London: 'Presumably if I'd been killed they would have contacted Keel's next of kin.'

Neville Taylor subsequently defended the action of his department in keeping the journalists off the Falklands: '[they] were not trained, were not equipped, were not familiarized, and we refused in London to issue instructions that they should be put ashore. We felt that that was a matter for the operational commanders on the spot to judge the moment when it was right.'

The 'Invincible Five' might well have stayed out at sea had they not, on 28 May, written a combined plea for help to their editors in London, which was eventually transmitted from *Invincible* three days later:

PRIORITY/PRIORITY 311548Z MAY 82
FROM HMS INVINCIBLE
TO MODUK
INFO CINCFLEET
RESTRICTED

Defence Press Office pse pass to editors named. Times, Guardian, Telegraph, the Sun and Daily Star. May 28 this is our situation since we went ashore two days ago with MoD approval. We were removed from the Falkland Islands by MoD and army press officers. . . . We are now on a supply ship in the Total Exclusion Zone, devoid of communications and have received through the captain a signal from MoD saying we must transfer to ships that are no longer in the area. The security aspects prevent further details other than to say we are effectively off the islands for at least the next ten days. . . . Our recommendation is that all pressure should be applied for equal treatment your correspondents and earliest return San Carlos Bay in interests our newspapers.

The message produced an immediate reaction in London. 'The level of thoughtlessness by your embarked press officers reaches a fresh zenith daily,' wrote Brian Hitchen of the *Daily Star* to Sir Frank Cooper on 1 June. 'I consider, Sir Frank, that the treatment of the press during the Falklands crisis has been shameful and have no doubt whatsoever that a full explanation will be called for at the appropriate time in the future.'

Cooper met Hitchen and the other editors at 6 p.m. that evening and promised to intervene on the reporters' behalf. The following day, Wednesday, 2 June, the 'Invincible Five' transferred to *Stromness*, which that night moved back inshore, and on 3 June the reporters finally landed. It was exactly two weeks since they had left *Invincible* to go ashore.

By contrast with their last brief visit, Port San Carlos was practically deserted, its only function now to act as a supply depot moving up stores for the final offensive. 'There was an awful feeling,' says Parry, 'of having missed the story.' That night the reporters slept in a sheep shed.

Even now they were still not properly equipped. Parry had some socks and boots and a sleeping bag which was not designed for Antarctic conditions. His main protection was an extremely uncomfortable waterproof suit. Moving around during the day caused a heavy sweat, and the moment the sun went down, 'there was the most terrible chill as the perspiration froze inside the suit.' Seamark, also poorly equipped, recalls nights spent shaking from head to foot with cold.

The following day, the 'Invincible Five' split up. McIlroy and Snow went south with the Guards, while Parry, Seamark and Witherow, joined by Richard Savill of the Press Association, made for Fitzroy, spending the night huddled in a garage. Parry's war was now very nearly over. Dispirited, exhausted, lacking the proper kit, he stayed on land for a few more days and then sought refuge on *Hermes*. He was given a place on a ship going back to Ascension and left before the Argentine surrender—the third journalist to drop out of the war before the end. 'It was the first campaign I had ever covered where my own kith and kin were fighting,' he reflected afterwards. 'And it was a complete disaster.'

It wasn't only the *Invincible* journalists who were kept off the Falklands.

'Cooped up on ship since landing,' Richard Savill signalled the Press Association in London. 'No access to shore. Slowly overcoming problem. *Canberra* press had it all. Hope for bite of cherry soonest.' Not until two weeks after the landings were Savill and PA photographer Martin Cleaver allowed permanently on shore.

A similar ban extended to the television journalists on *Hermes*. Brian Hanrahan said:

> My particular team, which was one of two television cameras there, were forbidden to leave the ship for about ten days or so after the landings had taken place. The argument was that they had too many people ashore and they did not want any more, and even to go ashore for a day and look around, we were told we could not do that.

The reason advanced by General Moore was that the television crew 'had not been training with our men on the way down, and with its heavy equipment and so on, moving about in the mountains, would probably have been a liability to itself and to my men to look after them'.

Covering the campaign on the Falkland Islands, as the *Canberra* journalists quickly discovered, was a gruelling experience. In other wars, correspondents can at least normally return after a few days at the front to a comfortable hotel. On the Falklands the journalists had to share many of the discomforts of the men twenty-four hours a day, seven days a week. Robert McGowan of the *Daily Express* was with 3 Para: 'I had to dig my own trench, cook all my own food, carry some of their mortar bombs for them—and lost 2 stone in weight doing so.' There were no cars, no beds, no canteens. Even a simple matter like having a cup of tea often involved breaking some ice off the top of a pond, melting it, adding water-purifying tablets, getting a small fire going and boiling it. Robert Fox called it 'the rat-pack war':

> When I say 'rat pack', I am borrowing the military abbreviation for 'rations pack', which we lived on solidly (the *mot juste* in the case of biscuits AB and AB fruit and compo paste) for days and weeks in the field. There was a small choice. First, you either had 'rats Arctic' or 'rats GS (General Service)', with a further

variation between menu 'A' and menu 'B', which meant either dehydrated chicken supreme or curry. According to the gourmets, the Arctic rats were better, but needed much more water, fine for Arctic snows, not so good in the Falklands, where the perils of liver fluke lurked in many of the streams.

Journalists went without such luxuries as a bath for weeks. The day before the Argentine surrender, a group of journalists on the side of Mount Kent were putting on delousing powder.

Kim Sabido recalled their experiences:

> If you were going to the front line, you had to walk and sleep in atrocious conditions. You had to be very fit. Your feet were just raw with walking. Several of us had to go back for treatment. Charles Lawrence of the *Sunday Telegraph* was taken back twice suffering from trench foot and exposure. Some people just withdrew into themselves and didn't even bother to push up to the front line.

'If you think you are getting frostbite,' an ex-SAS survival expert told Robert Fox, 'stick your toes in your oppo's crotch. It's the warmest part of his body, and that's your best chance.'

There were two basic forms of transport: by helicopter or on foot. Getting dispatches back to London in such conditions was often a matter of luck. Reports could be transmitted back to London only through the MARISAT ships inshore or through a Satellite Communications Centre capable of sending written copy, set up on land in a tent in Ajax Bay. This SATCOM facility was manned by Alan Percival—one of the few MoD minders for whom the journalists had a good word—who lived in some squalor in a tent alongside it. On one memorable occasion the entire SATCOM centre was blown away when a Chinook helicopter landed too close to it; it took several hours to restore it to working order.

The problem for the journalists, scattered with their units across hundreds of square miles of countryside, was to get their copy sent back to the transmission points. Robert McGowan explained:

> This particular war was unlike any other, in so far as you were with your unit. You could not just pop back to the local Intercontinental Hotel and file the copy; you lived in the trenches. Literally, you had to flag down a helicopter, put your copy into an envelope and ask that helicopter pilot if there was

any way he could get it to HMS *Fearless*, the central point for
vetting all press and TV copy. The pilots did a magnificent job
in that direction, but they had other priorities, so sometimes that
copy took a very long time to get to *Fearless*. . . .

Once cleared by the MoD PR officer on *Fearless*, reports then had
to be sent for transmission to MARISAT ships or to the SATCOM
centre in Ajax Bay. Frequently copy was lost. 'The first four
dispatches I attempted to file from the beachhead simply vanished
without trace,' claimed Ian Bruce of the *Glasgow Herald*. Richard
Savill listed five reports he'd written which never reached London: a
survivor's account of the Exocet attack on *Atlantic Conveyor*; copy on
the moonlit run by the requisitioned fishing boat *Monsoonan*;
Brigadier Wilson's account of the dash to occupy Bluff Cove; an
account of the battle for Mount Harriet; and a pooled piece from Port
Stanley, sent on the Monday night after the surrender.

When copy did manage to get through, it was invariably late.
Patrick Bishop wrote that 'the weight of military traffic on the only
land-based communications satellite meant that copy took a very low
priority and was taking up to twenty-four hours to transmit.' 'We
received some dispatches three or four days late,' said Michael
Reupke, Reuters' editor-in-chief. 'Sometimes the delay made the
reports unusable.'

Having been vetted once on the Falklands, copy was then censored
again in London. It was in the operation of this second filter, as Ian
McDonald had predicted, that the Ministry of Defence was accused
of making alterations on grounds of taste. The censors were military
officers working within the Ministry's Defence public relations staff.
'From 21 May onwards at least one of the military staff officers in
DPRS saw the embarked press's copy before it was passed to editors,'
stated the MoD. 'This vetting process within the MoD was carried
out as quickly as possible, and the average time taken to clear and
prepare dispatches for collection was under one hour.'

The censors mainly removed names of officers and men,
descriptions of the units involved in attacks and other military
details. But on some occasions they strayed into other areas. They
asked for the deletion of this section of a story on a field hospital filed
by Richard Savill:

> Surgeons working round the clock in the makeshift field
> hospital today carried out their hundredth major operation since

the fighting started. A total of 220 casualties have now been brought to the centre where four surgical teams are working in appalling conditions. As I toured the hospital—a disused refrigeration plant—the wounded were stretchered in from the battle front after arriving by helicopter. Many were wrapped in blood-soaked bandages. One bare-topped fatality was placed outside the building beneath a blue blanket. The casualties I saw were all Argentinians. Surgeon-Commander Rick Jolly, who is in charge, praised his team of surgeons working in dust and poor light. 'Despite the horrors of modern warfare, it is our proud boast here that everyone who has come in alive has gone out alive to the hospital.'

The censor, Wing-Commander Monks, gave his reasons for demanding the deletion of this passage in a note to the PA editor:

We are concerned that this story will cause a great deal of worry in the families of British servicemen. They are likely to believe that hospital treatment is inadequate. Whereas we believe that Richard Saville [sic] was commenting on Argentine wounded neglected by their own people and recovered under difficult battlefield conditions.

We would be grateful if your treatment of this story could bear in mind our genuine wish to avoid unnecessary worry and suffering in families here at home.

Another example, which occurred later in the campaign, concerned some derogatory remarks made by John Shirley of the *Sunday Times* about the Guards of 5 Infantry Brigade:

Unlike the marines and paras, the Guards, it seems, have not been taking daily exercise. They have complained about the food and grumbled about their cabins. One man is rumoured to have suffered a heart attack running up stairs. They are not liked. Nor, for that matter, is the captain of the *QE2*. Despite the fact that he had forty-two days' rations on board, the story is that he would not release any stores before sailing back to Ascension Island.

Lt.-Colonel Stephenson at the Ministry of Defence ordered that the whole paragraph be omitted on the grounds that this information 'would be very useful to the enemy'. Another section of the same dispatch, referring to the 'chagrin' of troops on the Falklands that the bodies of men killed might not be sent home, was to be omitted, 'as it could rekindle the worries of the bereaved'.

Patrick Bishop suspected that Ministry of Defence officials, both in London and in the Falklands, 'stifled any suggestion that the campaign was doing anything but rolling inexorably towards victory'. He later gave some examples to the House of Commons Defence Committee:

> On Thursday, 27 May, I wrote an article saying that the British advance was in danger of being bogged down and quoted senior officers to this effect. By the time this was released in London the references had been removed and the piece began about halfway through on a more optimistic note. On Wednesday, 9 June, I wrote an article quoting extensively survivors' accounts of the loss of the *Sir Galahad*, which made it clear that the ship was given inadequate protection and that there was anger and bitterness over the incident. I handed it to the MoD Press Officer Martin Helm, but when I saw him again five days later, after that week's edition of the paper had been published, he told me that it hadn't been sent. . . . The suppression of the piece was a simple act of censorship because it was felt the article might lower morale. In the event, there was little in the conduct of the war for the British forces to regret or feel ashamed of, but if there had been, it seems highly likely that nothing would have been allowed to be published about it while hostilities were in progress.

Occasionally, changes were made to reports somewhere along the line, without the reporters' knowledge, which deliberately altered the entire sense of the story. A line in a dispatch by John Shirley—'Only the weather holds us back from Stanley'—somehow became 'Only the *politicians* hold us back'. John Witherow found that a description he'd written of the 'failure' of the Vulcan bombing raids on Stanley was changed to read how 'successful' they were. One of the MoD minders claims that 'a certain lieutenant-colonel on the Falklands used to rewrite whole paragraphs relating to the Scots Guards which he didn't like.' The minder would wait until he'd gone and then change them back again.

Many of these problems arose because the journalists were wholly dependent upon the military for their communications. They were rarely around to see their copy transmitted— they were tens of miles away, dug in on a hillside or marching with their units. The reporters had to rely on the honesty of the authorities. The number of stories which went missing or were altered suggests that the military and the MoD were always ready to 'improve the image' of the war wherever possible. When Robert Fox reported on the disaster at Bluff Cove in which *Sir Galahad* and *Sir Tristram* were attacked, with heavy loss of life, he was

> enjoined by the MoD PRO in charge, Martin Helm, 'to print only the good news', i.e. that eleven Mirages had been shot down, allegedly, that day. Eventually even he realized the impossibility of such a policy and that every and any report emanating from the Force would have to lead on the Bluff Cove bombings.

The reporter who was most successful in his coverage of the war was the journalist most willing to report only the 'good news'. When Max Hastings of the London *Standard* was asked after the war whether he thought his positive approach had helped him, he replied: 'It may have done. It'd be foolish to deny it. Obviously the task force is more likely to give help to those whom they think are writing helpful things than those who are not.'

Almost all the journalists came to identify to a greater or lesser extent with the forces around them. 'The world of the Falklands campaign was so enclosed,' wrote Robert Fox, 'that it was hard not to identify with the troops on the ground; in the heavier engagements it was the only means of psychological survival.' Hastings subscribed to this view to a much greater degree. 'I've always had an enormous affection for the British Army and for the British forces,' he told *Panorama* after the war. 'I felt my function was simply to identify totally with the interests and feelings of that force.' He was asked whether, if morale were low, he would censor himself. 'Absolutely, absolutely.... When one was writing one's copy one thought: beyond telling everybody what the men around me are doing, what can one say that is likely to be most helpful to winning this war?' So great was Hastings's commitment to the cause that on 1 June he was allowed to use SAS satellite communications to dictate a report about them direct to their headquarters at Hereford: an unprecedented gesture from such an elite and secretive regiment.

Hastings, a lanky, bespectacled figure in his mid-thirties, is a military historian (author of the much-acclaimed *Bomber Command*) as well as a reporter used to covering the world's conflicts. 'Anybody with experience of war corresponding knows one has to be obsessed with communications,' he explained later. 'You need to treat problems of communication as if they were matters of life and death.' While most of the other reporters were content to stay with the units to which they had been assigned at the time of the landings, Hastings broke the rules, striking out and spending a few days with different units all over the island. He said later:

> We were all urged by the Ministry of Defence people that what we must do was stay with our units from beginning to end of the war . . . and some journalists very honourably did precisely that. I never felt—and again I said on *Canberra*—there was going to be an Eagle Scout badge at the end of the campaign for who suffered most. What is going to count is who got the most out, so one simply had to move from unit to unit according to who was doing something. When 42 Commando were going up Mount Kent I went with them, and again up Mount Harriet. I went on one of the frigates, and then in the build-up I was allowed to write about one of the helicopter squadrons, so that one simply had to move around units where something was going on. But I think it was true that those who actually obeyed instructions felt afterwards most betrayed. For instance, at one point 45 Commando were about to carry out an attack on Mount Kent, and we were told that the only way, if we wanted to join the attack (that is, myself and Robert Fox of the BBC), was to go yomping with them and we joined them. They had been already yomping for three days with their dispatch correspondents and they were already very tired. We yomped with them for another two days up Mount Kent, then when we got up Mount Kent, the first person I saw was Brigadier Thompson. I said, 'Looking forward to the attack tomorrow night?' and he looked astonished and said, 'Not tomorrow night, there'll not be an attack. We'll be lucky if we get one in a week.' So I simply shrugged my shoulders, hitched a ride back in a helicopter, and said to the others, 'I don't see any point in sitting on Mount Kent for a week. One can't file useful dispatches just sitting up here.'

Wherever Hastings went, he wrote. 'Every time I passed him,' says Kim Sabido, 'he was sitting in a greenhouse, surrounded by tomatoes, a little cigar in his mouth, hammering away at a portable typewriter balanced on his knee.' Hastings produced a stream of articles, concentrating not so much on being first with the news—which was where many of his Fleet Street colleagues made their mistake—but on writing 'colour' pieces about everything around him.

> I felt the most important thing was to start writing stories about every aspect of the task force, whether it was frigates, the air war, helicopter pilots or whatever. I just started moving around on my own doing these things and actually I was ticked off several times by MoD press officers for doing so much moving around, but I thought that they by then had proved themselves quite incapable and unsuited to organize any facilities for the journalists, and therefore it was entirely up to us to organize any facilities for ourselves. When it came to filing copy, whenever it was humanly possible I went physically to a ship in order to punch the tape myself. On the odd occasions when I did not do so, when like many others I handed helicopter pilots my copy, it was never seen again, and I do not blame the helicopter pilots for that.

Hastings loathed the MoD minders more than any other reporter: they impeded him in his headlong flight for copy. Virtually all the correspondents disliked the public relations men. They 'were held,' claimed Patrick Bishop, 'in equal contempt by journalists and task-force members alike.' But it was Hastings who decided to make his anger known publicly, in an article written at the beginning of the second week in June. Tailored specifically for the *Standard*'s Londoner's Diary, the piece claimed that 'among the correspondents animosity towards the Argentines is nothing like as bitter as towards the Ministry of Defence public relations department.'

> The most pitiful figures in all this are the Ministry public relations men on the spot, the minders as they are known without affection among the reporters. Not an impressive group from the first, since the task force entered the war zone these unhappy bureaucrats have become mere flotsam drifting meaninglessly from ship to ship, occasionally enforcing the latest restrictions from London, earning equal contempt from both reporter and military.

The final straw for the exhausted hack coming back to the ship from the mountains is to discover the minders, who pass their days reading newspapers in the wardroom, comfortably ensconced in their bunks, while the hacks doss down in sleeping bags on the floor. Retribution is promised when hostilities are over.

At the foot of this fulmination, Hastings added a note to the Diary's staff: 'I am most anxious that this is used in the hope of punitive action later.'

Before transmitting the article back to the UK, two of the minders attached their own comments to it, addressed to the Ministry of Defence. Senior press officer Martin Helm referred to 'Hastings's latest epic ... an inaccurate distortion written in a fit of pique at being denied access to the phone'. Alan George, an MoD PR with whom Hastings had just had an argument about communications, added his own terse postscript for Neville Taylor: 'Grateful you contact my solicitor, Mr R. Wilson of Chethams, 19 Buckingham Street, London, to consider whether Hastings's piece is actionable, and please advise us all accordingly.' When the various messages reached London, the Ministry of Defence—inexplicably, and to the anger of Helm and George—released the entire text of all three for publication. The war between press and press officers, hitherto private, was now out in the open.

The minders are still seething about the Hastings incident, in particular the imputation that they were little short of cowards, sheltering in comfort well out of danger. 'Alan George sat through every air attack in San Carlos Water,' says one, 'the only person—minder or journalist—to do so. So when Hastings wrote what he did, Alan was a bit miffed, to put it mildly. He'd hardly had any sleep—he'd been bombed for eight days.'

It wasn't only the minders who were irritated. Hastings—grabbing 'all sorts of means of transport—small boats, moving constantly'—also became increasingly unpopular with a large section of the press contingent on the Falklands. It gradually dawned upon some of the harder-bitten journalists that the Old Carthusian, Oxford-educated Hastings, so much more like one of the officers than a reporter, was beating them out of sight. Under a pooling arrangement, the press in London drew freely on the reports of one another's journalists, and Hastings's by-line dominated the newspapers: sometimes his stories even pushed out the dispatch from the paper's own correspondent. There were murmurings in the Falklands about 'favouritism', while in London the newspapers of the Express group, for whom Hastings worked, were jubilant about the success of their man. 'Only two names have dominated the Falklands war,' boasted the *Sunday Express*, 'Galtieri and Max Hastings.' That, commented Robert Fox, 'seems to cover a rather narrow political spectrum'.

Hastings's popularity among his colleagues reached its nadir in the final hours of the war, when he achieved his greatest coup: he became the first journalist to enter Port Stanley. The whole sequence of accidents, confusion and over-zealous military security which made up the last day of the land campaign proved a fitting climax to the whole war.

At midday on 14 June, with the British forces on the outskirts of Port Stanley, word spread that there were white flags flying over the capital. Max Hastings, naturally, was with the unit farthest forward, 2 Para, and the road into Stanley beckoned ahead. 'It was simply too good a chance to miss,' he wrote.

> Pulling off my web equipment and camouflaged jacket, I handed them to Roger Field in his Scimitar, now parked in the middle of the road and adorned with a large Union Jack. Then with a civilian anorak and a walking stick that I had been clutching since we landed at San Carlos Bay, I set off towards the town. . . .

Forty minutes later, having pretended to be from *The Times* and having talked to an Argentinian colonel, Hastings walked back into the British lines 'with the sort of exhilaration that most reporters are lucky enough to enjoy a few times in a lifetime.' His main priority now was to get back to *Fearless* and persuade the MoD minders to transmit the story immediately. 'When I came out of Stanley, Brigadier Thompson, extremely kind, realizing one had a marvellous scoop, arranged a helicopter for me to get back to the fleet to file my copy.' After 'a frenzied half-hour wait', during which Hastings tried to get on board three successive helicopters, the transport ordered by the brigadier arrived. Other reporters were milling around the British line, and Robert McGowan, Alastair McQueen, Derek Hudson, Ian Bruce and Leslie Dowd gave Hastings a 'pooled' dispatch they had written on the surrender for him to give to the MoD minders on *Fearless*; David Norris handed him a separate dispatch.

Hastings arrived at *Fearless* a few minutes before 4 p.m. local time 'to collect one of the Ministry of Defence public relations men'.

> I ran headlong into their cabin to seize one bodily and take him with me to a ship with transmission facilities. But I blurted out the essentials of my story to a disinterested audience. 'I am afraid that there is a complete news blackout,' declared the most senior of their number, a Mr Martin Helm. 'You cannot communicate at all until further notice.' Could he, I asked after an initial seizure, contact the Ministry to demand the lifting of the ban? No, such a call was covered by the ban itself.

What had happened was that John Nott had given instructions that no press were to be allowed to file copy. 'There was,' said Neville Taylor, 'an understandable and natural desire in London that that sort of announcement should be made first in London, preferably in Parliament.' There was an additional fear that a 'premature' disclosure from the Falklands might 'prejudice' the formal surrender negotiations which had not yet begun. Helm received a signal from Sir John Fieldhouse in which he was 'categorically told nothing could go back'.

> A bitter argument followed [wrote Hastings], in which it was put to him that Argentinian radio was already announcing a ceasefire, and that it was quite impossible to conceive what injury to British security might be done by a dispatch reporting my visit to Port Stanley. Mr Helm and his colleagues were unmoved. I went miserably to bed, to lie sleepless with rage towards the system which had so effortlessly thwarted me.

Brian Hanrahan, Michael Nicholson and their television crew were on Two Sisters Mountain when news of the white flags flying over Stanley came through. Hanrahan described what happened next:

> We went back to the brigade headquarters and saw the helicopter tasker there and tried to arrange the helicopters to split, so that Bernard Hesketh could go up into Stanley in order to film what was the end of the hostilities and I could head back to *Fearless* in order to send out reports and catch up with

Bernard the next morning. At that moment, an officer came along and said that the order from Commander Land Forces Falkland Islands was that no journalist was to be allowed into Stanley and neither was a journalist to be helped—I think that was his word—to get back to *Fearless*. We had a disagreement about what the word 'helped' meant. His interpretation was that we were not to go back to *Fearless*: mine was that they should not divert helicopters to take me to *Fearless*.

Faced with this total refusal to 'help', there was nothing for the television men to do but to set off down the side of the mountain on foot. Every time a helicopter went by, they waved at it frantically, until eventually one stopped.

It was a small Scout helicopter [recalled Nicholson], which should only take two passengers, but the sergeant pilot got five in the back, including our camera, all our burdens, our haversacks, and the crewman stood outside on the skids, and we got over to Fitzroy that way at 10 mph.

Like Hastings, Nicholson could scarcely believe it when Helm told him about the news blackout.

I was on *Fearless* at ten to ten. With *News at Ten* I had ten minutes to go with this incredible story of the end of the war.... Most of it was merely descriptive passages of how Stanley was taken and the war looked as if it was over and tonight the General was in Stanley negotiating a ceasefire. We could not see how that could in any way jeopardize the ceasefire negotiations....

While Nicholson and Hastings argued with Helm, Mrs Thatcher was announcing the news in the House of Commons: 'They are reported to be flying white flags over Port Stanley.' Once again, the war correspondents suffered the frustration of hearing the news announced over the World Service, without being able to do anything but hope to follow up with their own eyewitness accounts much later.

A little over two hours later, at 8.30 p.m. Falklands time (12.30 a.m. in London), General Moore arrived by helicopter at Government House in Port Stanley to conduct the surrender negotiations with the Argentine commander, General Menendez. It was a moment of triumph, mingled with great anxiety in case anything should go wrong. Moore had already forbidden any reporters to set foot in Stanley and was horrified to learn of Max Hastings's escapade earlier that afternoon.

Outside Government House the ubiquitous Martin Helm was on hand with two official photographers, and he asked Moore if he was willing to have the surrender filmed. 'I said "No",' recalled Moore.

> My reasoning was, and remains, that I was concerned with only one thing, and that was obtaining a surrender. I felt if there was half of a tenth of a 1 per cent chance that having the thing filmed might put Menendez off surrendering, and I did not know him, it would be a risk it could not be proper for me to take, and on those grounds I said 'No'.

It was a tense meeting. 'We were in a very poor way by 14 June,' stated Admiral Woodward. 'He was down to six rounds per gun that night; I had three frigates badly situated in terms of capability; we were running out of speed.' Sir Terence Lewin was listening to a running commentary on the negotiations on an open line to the Ministry of Defence, routed through SAS communications via Hereford.

Outside the negotiating room, Helm was waiting with his two official photographers—one from HMS *Fearless*, the other a Royal Marine commander—in the hope of getting a picture of the surrender being signed. But before Helm had a chance to get a picture of any sort, General Menendez agreed to capitulate and left, unescorted, with his officers. 'It was so quick,' explained Helm, 'we did not realize they were leaving.' Helm went in to see Moore and asked if it might be possible to get Menendez back in for a quick photography session: 'He said that unfortunately it was too late. They had already left.' For the first time in a modern conflict Britain had failed to get a single picture of her moment of triumph. Nor was a film cameraman or any journalist allowed to witness the evening of victory in Port Stanley. 'Posterity did not feature too much,' summed up David Nicholas.

Back on *Fearless*, Max Hastings was roused from his bed at 3 a.m. London time to be told that the news blackout, which had lasted for ten hours, had now been lifted. Refusing to trust the MoD minders to do anything, he made his way to the communications room and personally telexed to London the story of his triumphant march into Stanley.

What of the other copy, entrusted to him that afternoon by his fellow journalists? Hastings swears he gave it to one of the minders immediately he had punched out his own story. 'Fortunately, I took the precaution of doing so in the presence of a witness.' Although David Norris's piece eventually made it to London, the 'pooled' report by Robert McGowan and his colleagues disappeared: what happened to it remains a mystery to this day.

The absence of other stories enhanced the impact of Hastings's dispatch. It was the biggest scoop of the war, so complete that to its author it very nearly proved fatal. The other reporters were furious when they heard what had happened. At the Upland Goose, Port Stanley's hotel, Max Hastings was confronted by an angry Ian Bruce. According to one eyewitness:

> Max was sitting by the piano, when Bruce started yelling at him in a loud Glaswegian accent, which translated into something like, 'Hastings, you have lost my story and now I am going to kill you,' and then he pulled out an Argentinian bayonet. Patrick Bishop's face was one of studied amusement as to where Bruce would plunge the dagger. Then Derek Hudson piped up and said, 'This is neither the time nor the place to murder Max Hastings,' and Bruce was dragged off him. Poor Max went very white.

After a few days the owner of the Upland Goose actually refused to take journalists as guests. He told Alan Percival he was going to complain to the Press Council. The correspondents, he said, were 'worse than the Argies'.

In the last week of the war, Kim Sabido, the young reporter for Independent Radio News, filed a story that was bitterly critical of the media's behaviour on the Falklands. 'We have all been acting to a smaller or larger degree like overblown egos auditioning for parts in some awful B war movie,' Sabido told his listeners, and described how one minder had told him, 'If I had a pound for every time I've read "I dived for cover" or "The bomb burst just a few feet away", I'd be rich.' Sabido accused some reporters of outright lying— 'perpetrated, I believe, in a blind desire to be first with the news instead of just trying to be truthful'— and alleged two particular instances of reporters fabricating stories: 'those journalists who claimed to have read through binoculars street names in Stanley when still 10 miles behind the front line and within sight of nothing more than an Arctic ration pack', and the broadcaster who 'described in graphic detail how planes cartwheeled across the sky in the first dogfight of the war when he was, according to colleagues, locked below decks some 80 miles from the action'.

There were other examples of bogus stories which Sabido didn't quote. One 'eyewitness account' of the rescue of survivors from Bluff Cove was, swear the minders, broadcast by a journalist who was further up the coast with a large hill between himself and Bluff Cove at the time. Another reporter filed a false story about motorcycles being fitted with rocket launchers. Some journalists listened to broadcasts on the World Service, rewrote them and sent them back to their newspapers as if they were first-hand accounts. Five reporters arrived to cover the attack on Mount Kent with their reports on the action already written, based upon an inaccurate briefing: they had described the assault as having been preceded by a 'heavy bombardment', when in fact the plan was to mount a silent attack. The journalists held a hurried meeting. Two of the reporters were unhappy, but the consensus was to let the inaccurate stories—by now on their way to *Fearless* for clearance—be transmitted unchanged.

'When the final roll of honour comes to be drawn up for both British and Argentines alike,' said Sabido, 'I would humbly suggest that with some very noble exceptions . . . we the reporters will not be on that list.' Sir Frank Cooper gave vent to some justified exasperation to the Commons Defence Committee:

> I have not seen or heard a single admission, if I may say so—and I am not being beastly to the media—that any of them got anything wrong or that every single correspondent was not a knight in shining armour riding a white horse in search of the absolute truth.

After the war, Surgeon-Commander Morgan O'Connell, a psychiatrist sailing with the task force, described in the *Guardian* the symptoms of battle stress that he noticed in the men under his care: 'emotional tension, hypersensitivity to noise, explosive rage, a feeling of helplessness, amnesia and regression to childish behaviour'. Of all the groups during the war he found that the journalists fared the worst: 'They had no group cohesiveness. They were in competition with each other all the time, so they couldn't draw the same security from their group.'

Out of the twenty-eight correspondents who started with the task force, three dropped out, suffering from varying degrees of strain. Few of those left in Port Stanley at the end of the war had any desire to remain on the islands for a day longer than necessary. John Witherow and Patrick Bishop have described some of the ploys considered by the journalists in order to get off the Falklands quickly:

> chartering a seaplane from Chile, taking a hospital ship with the casualties to Montevideo and, most far-fetched of all, trying to leave via Argentina with the prisoners on *Canberra*. Others boarded RFA *Resource* with the assurance she would reach Ascension within a week. The captain explained that his none-too-swift ammunition ship would have to do 35 knots to arrive in that time. Nevertheless, a number embarked and once at sea were told there had been a change of plan and they were bound for South Georgia. They managed to get a helicopter back to Stanley.

A straw poll was held to allocate seats on the first Hercules flight back to the UK; when it was completed, the list of successful journalists was stolen and hidden behind the bar. Offers of hundreds of pounds were made for a seat; none was accepted.

Most reporters were glad to have covered the war, but few wished to repeat the experience. Brian Hanrahan said he would 'probably be quite pleased' to be asked, 'but I am not sure I would be altogether pleased to go through it all again'. Hastings, characteristically, was more positive.

> One felt an enormous sense of privilege to have the opportunity to be there. After so many years in which one has been reporting on one aspect or another of national failure, it was enormously moving to see and to record a national success. Whether the war should have been fought at all, whether it was necessary, whether it was a good thing—one is almost dismayed to have to think about those things because you lose that magical sense one had in Stanley when the war ended. You thought, Gosh, one's actually taken part in a great British success. And it is saddening to come back to the real world.

Robert Fox echoed the same sentiments:

> One feels mildly affronted for it to be suggested that such an extraordinary experience, which so nearly cost me my life, was

worthless. The days in that wild landscape, the companionship of many of the men in the field were enjoyable more often than not; fear and danger were exhilarating too. . . . *For me it was an existential dream*. [Author's emphasis.]

Around 1,000 British servicemen were killed or wounded during the Falklands campaign; Argentina suffered over 1,800 casualties. Yet the final and dominant impression of the media's coverage of the war is its unreality.

In part this was a reflection of the nature of the conflict itself. The *Observer*'s Neal Ascherson described an editorial conference in London as divided between 'those who thought something real was taking place and those who assumed they were having a gaudy dream'.

As the Falklands war ended, the Israelis attacked Lebanon. Night after night, British television carried pictures of suffering and destruction. Yet images of death and injury hardly featured at all in the media's coverage of the fighting in the South Atlantic.

To take one example: on 27–8 May, 250 Argentine soldiers were killed in a *single* attack, yet, as Peter Preston, editor of the *Guardian*, pointed out, 'We had pictures of Argentinian helmets on bayonets after Goose Green but not a body in sight throughout.' The first television film of British casualties following Goose Green was not transmitted for over two weeks: ironically, it was shown on 14 June, the night Mrs Thatcher announced the cease-fire, and followed pictures of her appearance in Downing Street listening to patriotic crowds singing 'Rule Britannia'.

The media also played their part in converting the war into what Bishop and Witherow described as a 'national drama' with 'all the cathartic effect of a Shakespearean tragedy'. Lieutenant David Tinker, a 25-year-old officer on HMS *Glamorgan*, described one encounter with the media at the time of the Pebble Island raid on 14 May:

The BBC were on board and grandiosed everything out of all proportion (Antarctic wind, Force 9 gales, terrific disruption done, disruption of entire Argentinian war effort, etc.). Mostly, they sat drinking the wardroom beer and were sick in the Heads: the weather was in fact quite good.

More than 1,000 men lost their lives in the struggle for the Falklands. Tinker was one of them—killed along with twelve other members of *Glamorgan*'s crew when she was hit by an Exocet missile on 12 June.

> The newspapers just see it as a real-life 'War Mag' [he wrote on 28 May] and even have drawings of battles, and made-up descriptions, entirely from their own imagination! If some of the horrible ways that people died occurred in *their* offices, maybe they would change their tone. Let us hope it ends quickly.

Conclusion

Closing the Emergency Press Centre on 18 June, Ian McDonald told reporters that he had found the past ten weeks 'totally engrossing and tremendously exciting' and ended by quoting Prospero's final speech in *The Tempest*:

> Now my charms are all o'erthrown,
> And what strength I have's mine own,
> Which is most faint. . . .

That afternoon Ian McDonald left public relations for good. Three weeks later he took up a new post as head of the Adjutant General's secretariat.

Michael Nicholson celebrated his return home by buying a new house in a tiny village in Sussex. It became commonplace, as the weeks went by after the end of the war, to say that the media and the Navy must put the bitterness of the campaign behind them and learn to live together. The phrase took on a new shade of meaning for Nicholson, who has discovered that his neighbour in that enclosed community is the captain of *Hermes*—Lyn Middleton.

Six of the reporters who sailed with the task force either wrote or collaborated on books about the Falklands. Patrick Bishop and John Witherow wrote *The Winter War*; John Shirley contributed to the Insight book *The Falklands War*; Max Hastings joined Simon Jenkins to write *Battle for the Falklands*; Robert Fox wrote *Eyewitness Falklands*, and he and Brian Hanrahan had their dispatches from the South Atlantic published as a book by the BBC. 'Never in the field of human conflict', commented one reviewer, 'has so much been written by so many so quickly.'

Seventeen task-force correspondents gave oral or written evidence to the House of Commons committee investigating the MoD's handling of the media. Over a period of five months, under the benign gaze of the committee's chairman, Sir Timothy Kitson, the protagonists of the information war paraded in front of MPs.

A few scenes linger in the memory. Dr John Gilbert, a junior Defence Minister in the last Labour Government, cross-examining Sir Frank Cooper and accusing him of '*suppressio veri suggestio falsi*— suppression of the truth and the suggestion of what is false, in the course of which you do not tell a single lie', with Cooper bristling at what he called an 'obnoxious suggestion'. Max Hastings, beaming with pleasure at the recollection of his triumphs while at the same time trying to look modestly at the floor. Brian Hanrahan's quiet accusations of news management: 'I am sure there were times when information was messed about for reasons which had nothing to do with military information.' Admiral Woodward's opinion of the minder on *Hermes*—'I am a great believer in setting a thief to catch a thief. I am not sure whether Mr Hammond was a thief in press affairs', a comment which revealed as much about the Navy's attitude to the media as a volume of evidence. Finally there was the undisguised irritability of Sir Terence Lewin at having to give an account of himself to the committee: 'We won, which I assume was what the Government and the public and the media all wanted us to do.... I am somewhat surprised that there is a need now to have this great post mortem into the media aspects of the campaign in the South Atlantic.' 'I do not think,' replied Kitson, 'we should get into a discussion this afternoon as to whether it is right to hold an inquiry.'

The wounds caused by the Falklands war did not heal quickly— least of all those inflicted within the Ministry of Defence. In October an internal MoD document was leaked to the Commons committee revealing that guidelines *had* been drawn up as early as 1977 to deal with the media in 'situations of crisis and increased tension ... outside a NATO context'. The paper, entitled 'Public Relations Planning in Emergency Operations', laid down details of 'responsibilities for co-ordination' within the MoD PR department, and its recommendations had a specific relevance to the Falklands crisis:

> For planning purposes it is anticipated that twelve places would be available to the media, divided equally between ITN, BBC and the press.... The press should be asked to give an undertaking that copy and photographs will be pooled. Within the overall seat allocation and bids from the media every effort should be made to include a radio reporter in the party.

As the Ministry had been insisting that—in Cooper's words—'there was no pre-planning' for coping with the media in a Falklands-style operation, the revelation of this five-year-old contingency plan caused considerable embarrassment. Ian McDonald was forced to confess that he had never even heard of it. It had been leaked by the Army deliberately to give the despised 'administrators' within the MoD a rough time. 'It was done by the Green Jackets,' claims one furious official, 'the biggest shits in Britain.'

The Defence Committee was also encountering divisions within the media. The MPs discovered that Cooper's non-attributable briefings were all recorded by the MoD and asked for the tapes to be released. Neville Taylor, 'mending fences' and 'trying to establish better relations and a better understanding' with the media, consulted the defence correspondents concerned, and *they* voted by nine to seven not to give the committee access to the tapes. Taylor explained that they had 'expressed the view that the principle was important'. Timothy Kitson was angry and exasperated: 'Here we are inquiring into the problems, trying to be helpful to the media, doing all we possibly can to be reasonable about this inquiry, and then we find they are consulted about some tapes which, in fact, we are entitled to see and should see. . . .' The committee had run up against the symbiotic relationship, fostered by the lobby system, which had allowed misinformation to be so easily planted in the first place.

The Falklands conflict may well prove the last war in which the armed forces are completely able to control the movements and communications of the journalists covering it. Technology has already overtaken the traditional concepts of war reporting. The combination of lightweight video cameras and commercial satellites may mean that commanders will hear news of fighting as quickly through watching television as through normal military sources. 'You will never have it easier than the Falklands,' Sir Frank Cooper told the Commons Defence Committee:

> If any of us sit down and think for a moment that if there was a Soviet incursion into some part of Europe, what would actually happen in terms of war, diplomacy and the media, I think we would all find very great difficulty in answering all those questions to anybody's satisfaction at the moment. Obviously,

we shall need to look at the whole question of whether there should be some form of censorship. Is any form of censorship practical in the modern world? It is highly unlikely we would get anything as simple as that again in a real shooting-type war.

'In a few years' time,' said John Nott, 'I think the task of censorship, with satellites, will become an impossible one.' The British Government might be able to impose censorship on British satellite stations. It cannot expect to control foreign or international ones. If Britain were to be involved in joint military action with the Americans, would one population be given more information than the other? How could any censorship authority keep track of the sheer volume of material being transmitted from the battlefield and from capitals around the world?

I think the only conclusion I can safely reach [said Cooper] is that nobody has thought about this in anything like the depth that needs to be done to try and find out answers to difficult questions. Indeed, there are no simple or short answers to any of these issues. These are major and fundamental questions which will have a bigger impact on any kind of warfare than we have ever supposed to be the case.

The Ministry of Defence is setting up a committee to investigate the subject, under the chairmanship of 'a distinguished retired general'. Its terms of reference are 'To consider—not least in the light of the Falklands operation—whether any new measures, including the introduction of a system of censorship, are necessary to protect military operations....' The MoD has also decided to sponsor a two- or three-year research project that will study the relationship between the armed forces and the media in time of war.

But this concentration on the long-term implications of censorship should not divert attention from the central lesson of the 'information war'. The episodes which caused the most disquiet, and which have been described in this book, were not necessarily unique to the Falklands crisis. The instinctive secrecy of the military and the Civil Service; the prostitution and hysteria of sections of the press; the lies, the misinformation, the manipulation of public opinion by the authorities; the political intimidation of broadcasters; the ready connivance of the media at their own distortion . . . all these occur as much in normal peace time in Britain as in war.

The Falklands crisis had one unique and beneficial side-effect. Its limited time-scale and crowded succession of incidents made it an experience of great intensity. It briefly illuminated aspects of British society usually hidden from view. It *exposed* habitual abuses by the armed forces, Government, Whitehall and the media; it did not *create* them. And although the war itself is over, the fighting here goes on: its first casualty—as always—truth.

Index

Ad Hoc Falkland Islands Peace
  Committee, 87
Adley, Robert, 75, 76
Alexander, Andrew, 39
Andrew, Prince, 28–9, 46
Archer, Peter, 21, 22, 121, 122
Arlen, Michael J., 64
Arrow, 65
Ascension Island, 17, 34, 35, 37, 59,
  61
Ascherson, Neal, 146
Ashton, Ken, 51
Atkins, Humphrey, 16

Barratt, Robin, 21, 31, 34
Beetham, Sir Michael, 78
Benn, Tony, 45, 81, 87
Biffen, John, 67, 86, 87
Biggs-Davison, John, 84
Bishop, Patrick, 23, 120, 121, 125,
  127, 132, 134, 137, 143, 145, 146,
  148
Black, Captain Jeremy, 28, 30, 31,
  32, 34–6, 47, 64, 92, 123–4
Bluff Cove, 61, 118, 135, 144
Bottomley, Horatio, 50
Braine, Sir Bernard, 81, 92
Bristol, HMS, 122
British Broadcasting Corporation
  (BBC), 13, 14, 16, 18, 22, 24, 35,
  57, 71, 73–91, 92, 119; attempts
  to get TV pictures from S.
  Atlantic, 57–9; and censorship,
  60–1; attacks MoD, 61, 70; and
sinking of *Sheffield*, 66–7; claims
  Argentina a credible source of
  news, 71; and Suez, 73; coverage
  attacked, 75–7, 79–85, 87;
  coverage defended, 85–6, 87;
  suspends Robert Kee, 86; public
  support for, 88–9
Bruce, Ian, 24, 132, 139, 143
Burne, Captain Cristopher, 25, 32

Caldwell, Brigadier F. G., 64
Cam Ne, 63
Campaign, 52–3
Canberra, 23, 24, 25, 26, 32, 37, 48,
  115, 120, 121, 124, 145
Carrington, Lord, 39, 86
censorship, 26–7, 60–1, 107–8, 121,
  132–4, 151
Central Office of Information
  (COI), 95, 101
Charles, Prince of Wales, 86, 87
Churchill, Winston, MP, 75, 84–5
Churchill, Winston (Prime
  Minister), 39, 73, 93
Clark, Alan, 84
Cleaver, Martin, 21, 130
Cockerell, Michael, 76, 77, 78, 80,
  88
Cole, John, 66
Collins, Captain Tony, 25, 26
Connell, Jon, 98
Conqueror, HMS, 108
Conservative Party, 14, 72, 83–4,
  86, 91

153

Cooper, Sir Frank, 19, 24, 26, 28, 72, 90, 96, 98, 101, 102, 129, 149; believed too many task-force reporters, 23; relieved at lack of TV pictures, 59; defends not telling 'the full truth', 70; regrets ending unattributable briefings, 107; replaces McDonald, 108–9; briefs editors, 109–10; briefs defence correspondents, 110–11; and San Carlos landings, 110–14; criticizes press, 144; and future problems of censorship, 150–1

Coventry, HMS, 114–16

Crawley, Eduardo, 76, 78

Crimea, 56

Critchley, Julian, 72, 88

Crouch, David, 76, 78

Cudlipp, Lord, 52

Daily Express, 19, 22, 29, 39, 42, 50, 82, 111

Daily Herald, 43

Daily Mail, 19, 22, 38, 39, 55, 75, 81, 82

Daily Mirror, 13, 19, 40, 41, 49, 51, 82, 85, 111; circulation war with *Sun*, 42–3; opposes task force, 43–4; loss of readers during Suez, 44; reaction to loss of *Sheffield*, 49; calls *Sun* 'the harlot of Fleet Street', 51–2; increases circulation, 54–5

Daily Star, 18, 20, 28, 41, 43, 97

Daily Telegraph, 19, 89, 100, 111–12

Dalyell, Tam, 76, 77, 81

Deedes, William 110

Defence Committee (House of Commons), 14, 58, 64, 68, 107, 112, 119, 126, 134, 148–51

Defford, 58

DISCUS, 58

Dowd, Leslie, 24, 139

Dunkley, Chris, 88

Eden, Anthony, 73

electronic newsgathering (ENG) 56–7, 59, 69

English, Michael, 51

Evans, Michael, 113

Fairhall, David, 98

Fearless, 121, 125, 132, 139, 140, 141, 142, 144

Fieldhouse, Sir John, 17, 18, 107–8, 114, 115, 116, 122, 140

Foot, Michael, 43, 52, 81

Foreign and Commonwealth Office (FCO), 16, 39, 97

Foreign Press Association, 24, 97

Foulkes, George, 76, 77, 81

Fox, Robert, 21, 32, 121, 130–1, 135, 136, 139, 145–6, 148

Francis, Richard, 67, 83, 84, 115–16

Gaitskell, Hugh, 73

General Belgrano, 13, 33, 108

George, Alan, 28, 138

Gibbard, Leslie, 49

Gilbert, Dr John, 70, 149

Glamorgan, HMS, 122, 146, 147

Glasgow Herald, 85

Glasgow Media Group, 87

Goodwin, Roger, 15, 21, 27, 28, 30, 31, 32, 35, 36, 48, 123, 124, 125–6

Goose Green, 117–18, 146

Grant, Anthony, 79

Griffiths, Eldon, 79

Grisewood, Harman, 73

Guardian, 13, 18, 20, 21, 38, 39, 44, 49, 50, 53, 85, 112, 144

Haines, Joe, 51–2

Hammond, Graham, 34, 68–9, 121

Hands, Jeremy, 121

Hanrahan, Brian, 20, 21, 22, 31, 32–4, 37, 55, 93, 130, 148, 149; dispatch on Bluff Cove censored, 61; and sinking of *Sheffield*, 65,

67; and Argentine surrender, 140–1, 145

Hastings, Max, 18, 24, 94, 100, 117, 121, 135–9, 148, 149; attack on minders, 137–8; first journalist to enter Port Stanley, 139–40, 141, 142; attempted murder of, 143; sums up feelings on campaign, 145

Heaps, Peter, 21, 57

Helm, Martin, 25, 28, 124, 134, 135, 138, 140, 141, 142

Hermes, HMS, 21, 30–1, 32, 34, 57, 99, 121

Hesketh, Bernard, 21, 33, 67, 69, 140–1

Hicks, Robert, 76

Hitchen, Brian, 18, 41, 45, 109, 110, 129

House of Commons, 16, 67, 116, 118

Howard, George, defends BBC policy, 75; and Tory Media Committee, 83–5; character, 84

Hudson, Derek, 139, 143

Hutchinson, Bob, 106, 113

Independent Radio News (IRN), 21, 120

Independent Television News (ITN), 18, 24, 90, 94, 104; and transmission of pictures from S. Atlantic, 57–8; criticizes MoD and Navy for 'lack of will', 59; attacks MoD's information policy, 105–6; and sinking of *Coventry*, 114–15

Information Co-ordination Group, 101–2

Ingham, Bernard, intervenes on press's behalf, 19–20; supports Neville Taylor, 96; co-ordinating role of, 101; critical of MoD, 116; and Goose Green, 117; and Bluff Cove, 118

Ingrams, Richard, 103

Intrepid, 121

Invincible, HMS, 21, 22, 27, 30, 31, 32, 34, 35, 48, 99, 122, 124

Jackson, Harold, 92

Jameson, Derek, 42, 43, 46, 109, 110

Jockell, John, 21

John Bull, 50

Jones, Colonel 'H', 117, 118

Kee, Robert, 76, 77, 78–9, 80; attacks *Panorama*, 86; resigns, 86–7

Kitson, Sir Timothy, 148, 149, 150

Knightley, Philip, 64

Latimer Defence College, 119

Lawrence, Charles, 131

Leach, Admiral Sir Henry, 15, 17, 69, 114, 115, 116

Leigh, David, 110

Le Page, John, 18–19

Lewin, Admiral Sir Terence, 17, 93, 142, 149; and deceiving the public, 94; importance of PR to, 102; unhappy with handling of PR, 105; and sinking of *Coventry*, 114–16; and Bluff Cove, 118

Llewellyn, Roddy, 16

lobby system, 110, 150

Longhurst, Commander P. H., 58

Lowe, Martin, 37

McDonald, Ian, 18, 57, 99, 113, 116, 132, 150; plan to fly correspondents to Ascension, 17, 23; and sinking of *Sheffield*, 66–7, 69–70; career of, 95, 96; abolishes unattributable briefings, 96–8, 110; and recapture of South Georgia, 99–100; daily statements of, 101–4; fame of, 103–4; centralization of power by, 106;

disagreements with Taylor, 106–9; loses overall control, 108–9; and sinking of *Coventry*, 115; leaves public relations, 148

McGowan, Robert, 22, 23, 29, 37, 121, 130, 131–2, 139, 143

McIlroy, Alfred J., 21, 35, 123, 124, 126, 127, 129

MacKenzie, Kelvin, 13, 44, 47; appointed editor of *Sun*, 42; character of, 42; and 'treason' editorial, 51, 53

McQueen, Alastair, 24–5, 27, 121, 139

MARISAT, 32–3, 123

Maude, Sir Angus, 82

Meacham, Jim, 62–3, 97, 100, 111, 112–13

Menendez, General Mario, 141–2

Menzies, Robert, 73

Meyer, Sir Anthony, 76, 78, 82

Middleton, Captain Lyn, 30–1, 33, 64, 108, 121, 148

Mills, Peter, 77, 79

Milne, Alasdair, 76, 83, 89; predicts attack on BBC, 73–4; and Tory Media Committee, 83–5, 88; character, 84

'minders' (MoD press officers), 27–8; 137–8

Ministry of Defence (MoD), 14, 15, 16, 18, 19, 20, 23, 24, 25, 30, 34, 90, 92–119, 122, 123, 138, 140; and transmission of TV pictures, 58–9, 60; fears of Vietnam, 64; criticized by Cabinet, 77; structure of PR department, 95–6; and recapture of South Georgia, 99–100; opens Emergency Press Centre, 101; divisions within PR department, 104–9; loses credibility, 113–14, 118–19; inquiry over Goose Green, 118; division with

Downing Street, 116, 118; and Bluff Cove, 118; MPs announce inquiry into, 119; operation of censorship, 132–4; continuing divisions within, 149–50; considers implications of Falklands crisis, 151

misinformation, 93, 113; during Second World War, 93

Molloy, Mike, 42–3, 54–5, 115; describes *Sun* as 'Christmas-cracker wrapping', 43; considers suing *Sun*, 51

Monroe, Sir Hector, 85

Moore, Maj.-Gen. Sir Jeremy, 60, 120–1, 130; fears of TV coverage, 62, 64; and Argentine surrender, 141–2

Mowrer, Paul Scott, 92

Mulley, Fred, 95

Murdoch, Rupert, 13, 41, 44

Narval, 123

National Union of Journalists (NUJ), 47, 51, 53, 54

News at Ten, 114, 115, 116, 141

News Chronicle, 43

Newsnight, 71–2, 74–5, 80, 89

News of the World, 18, 48

Newspaper Publishers' Association (NPA), 18–19

Newsweek, 63

Nicholas, David, 56, 57–8, 89, 90, 106, 142

Nicholson, Michael, 20, 21, 27, 28, 32–3, 55, 61, 93, 123; relations with Lyn Middleton, 30–1, 33, 108, 121; and sinking of *Sheffield*, 67–9; and *General Belgrano*, 108; threatened with 'sack', 121; and Pebble Island raid, 121–2; and Argentine surrender, 140–1; return home, 148

Nicolson, Harold, 73

Nine o'Clock News, 66–7

Norris, David, 21, 37, 121, 140, 143

Northwood (Fleet Headquarters), 17, 21, 23, 114

Nott, John, 19, 21, 24, 39, 59, 74, 96, 98, 102, 140, 151; and sinking of *Sheffield*, 66, 67; and sinking of *Coventry*, 114–16; and Goose Green, 117–18; and Bluff Cove, 118

Oakhanger, 57

Observer, 44, 85, 109, 114

O'Connell, Morgan, 144

Olmeda, 33, 123

Oppenheim, Sally, 80, 81

Page, John, 72, 74, 80

Paley, William, 87

Panorama, 76, 77–9, 80–1, 84–5, 86–7, 89, 92, 135

Parkinson, Cecil, 78, 101

Parry, Gareth, 20, 21, 22, 27, 32, 48, 122, 125, 126, 127, 128, 129

Pebble Island raid, 111, 121–2, 123, 146

Pentagon, 58

Percival, Alan, 21, 22, 23, 37, 126, 127, 131, 143

Port Stanley, recapture of, 139–43

Press Association, 19, 97, 118, 119, 122, 130

Preston, Peter, 51, 146

Protheroe, Alan, and transmission of TV pictures, 58–9; critical of Navy and MoD, 59, 95, 106

'psyops', 119

Pym, Francis, 16, 77, 87

Queen Elizabeth II, SS, 124, 133

Radio Atlantico del Sur, 119

Reform Club, 18

Resource, 124–6, 145

Reupke, Michael, 24, 113, 132

Reuters, 24

Rippon, Geoffrey, 79

Rocky Mountain News, 15

Rodgers, William, 87

Royal Navy, 16–17, 20, 21, 24, 33, 68–9

Sabido, Kim, 21, 26, 32, 37, 120, 125, 131, 136; critical of task-force correspondents, 143–4

Safer, Morley, 63

Salt, Captain Sam, 68, 70

SATCOM centre, 131, 132

Savill, Richard, 122, 129, 130, 132–3

Scoop, 110

SCOT, 57–8

Seamark, Michael, 20, 21, 28–9, 123, 126, 127, 129

Shawcross, Tim, 76, 80

Sheffield, HMS, 13, 49, 65–70, 122

Shirley, John, 125, 127, 133–4, 148

Sir Galahad, 118, 134, 135

Sir Geraint, 127

Sir Lancelot, 22, 29, 37

Sir Tristram, 118, 135

SKYNET, 58

Smith, Geoffrey Johnson, 85

Smith, Tom, 22, 37

Smith, Tony, 97

Snow, Peter, 50, 72, 75, 80

Snow, Tony, 20, 21, 27, 28–9, 47–8, 123, 126, 127, 129

South Georgia, 47, 56, 74, 99–100, 119

Spark, Ronald, 50, 53, 54

Special Air Service (SAS), 57, 99, 135, 142

Special Boat Section (SBS), 119

Standard, 18, 137

Steel, David, 87

Stephens, Peter, 41, 42, 45, 47, 48, 49, 51, 53, 55

Stokes, John, 82
Stromness, 22, 37, 125, 129
Suez, 26, 44, 55, 73
Sun, 13, 20, 28–9, 44–5, 75, 79, 82,
   83, 100, 112, 118; 'GOTCHA!'
   headline, 13, 47; attacks Lord
   Carrington, 39; recent history of,
   41–3; attacks *Daily Mirror*, 44–5,
   51, 53; calls Tony Benn 'a
   termite', 45; says 'Knickers to
   Argentina', 46; advises General
   Galtieri to stick it up his Junta,
   45–6; sponsors missile, 47–8;
   treats war as a game, 48; reaction
   to sinking of *Sheffield*, 49;
   accusations of treason, 50–1;
   attacked, 51–2; compared with
   Nazis, 52; asks 'Why all the
   fuss?', 53; intensifies support for
   task force, 54; loses circulation,
   54; denounced by Michael Foot,
   81
Sunday Express, 139
Sunday People, 110
Sunday Times, 44, 87
Superb, HMS, 98

Taylor, Neville, 128, 140, 150;
   difficulties of censoring TV, 60;
   appointed chief of public
   relations, 96, 104–5;
   disagreements with McDonald,
   104–9; takes control, 109; row
   with Bernard Ingham, 118
television, 55; delay in getting
   pictures back, 56; technical
   problems in transmitting
   pictures, 57–8; worries about
   effects of coverage, 59–60; and
   Vietnam, 61–4; effects of lack of

pictures, 70–1; future
   development of, 50–1
Thatcher, Margaret, 20, 39, 49, 50,
   89, 117, 141, 146; and sinking of
   Sheffield, 65–6; attitude to BBC,
   74; instructs media to 'Rejoice',
   74, 100; reaction to *Newsnight*,
   74–5; watches *Panorama*, 77–8;
   attacks *Panorama*, 80–1
Thompson, Brigadier Julian, 126,
   136, 139
The Times, 18, 20, 21, 38, 41, 56, 79,
   80, 85, 86, 87, 112
Tinker, Lt. David, 146–7
Trethowan, Sir Ian, 83, 85

Upland Goose, the, 143

Vietnam, 61–5
Viggers, Peter, 116

Waterhouse, Keith, 103
Wertham, Fredric, 64
Whitehouse, Mary, 79
Whitelaw, William, 85, 87
Wilson, Brigadier Tony, 64, 132
Witherow, John, 21, 30, 32, 37, 92,
   126, 127, 129, 134, 145, 146, 148
Woodward, Admiral Sir John, 64,
   111, 121, 142, 149; and sinking of
   Sheffield, 68, 69, 74; prepared to
   use media for misinformation, 93;
   and recapture of South Georgia,
   100
World Service (BBC), 16, 68, 73,
   123, 124, 128, 141, 144; and
   Goose Green, 117–18

Yarmouth, 65
Yorkshire Post, 85